D1155665

Steal My Heart

USA TODAY BESTSELLING AUTHOR

Heather B. Moore

Steal My Heart

A Prosperity Ranch Novel

Copyright © 2020 by Heather B. Moore
Print edition
All rights reserved

No part of this book may be reproduced in any form whatsoever without prior written permission of the publisher, except in the case of brief passages embodied in critical reviews and articles. This is a work of fiction. The characters, names, incidents, places, and dialogue are products of the author's imagination and are not to be construed as real.
Interior design by Cora Johnson
Edited by JL Editing Services and Lisa Shepherd
Cover design by Rachael Anderson
Cover image credit: Deposit Photos #157637254
Published by Mirror Press, LLC

ISBN: 978-1-947152-99-1

Steal My Heart

She's ready to leave Prosper behind, forever. So why did she have to meet him, of all times, and of all places? That was never the plan.

Disaster seems to follow Evie Prosper's dating life everywhere. A fresh start can only mean leaving Prosper forever, which is what she's determined to do, until she meets Carson Hunt. He unknowingly saves her from another dating disaster, yet their paths keep crossing. Carson is relocating to Prosper of all places, and if Evie could change that one thing about him, she might rethink their connection.

1

EVIE PROSPER SLAMMED HER dorm room door shut and flopped against it. "He asked me out. He asked me out! I think my luck has finally changed!"

"Okay, okay," Becca said with a laugh. "You don't need to shout."

Evie slid down the door until she was sitting with her knees drawn up to her chest. She closed her eyes for a moment, feeling the waves of excitement pulse through her. Devon, the star quarterback for their Texas college team, had finally asked her out. It had been weeks since they'd first started talking, and not that Evie expected Devon to be *the one*, as in marriage and happily ever after, but it was fun to dream.

Her eyes popped open. "Oh no." She scrambled to her feet and rushed to the narrow closet. "I'm meeting him in an hour. One hour! Sixty minutes!"

Becca groaned and shut down her laptop. "I'm out of here. Not really a fan of hyper Evie while she gets ready for a date by trying on every item of clothing in this dorm room."

Evie spun around to stare at her red-headed best friend and roommate. Becca was one of those girls who was beautiful

1

with no makeup, no primping. But Evie had never gone a day without makeup in public since she was about thirteen. Yeah, she knew she was a slave to her beauty routine, but if it got her dates with the likes of Devon, it was worth it.

"Are you seriously leaving?" Evie asked Becca when she was halfway to the door.

Becca paused with a hand on the doorknob and turned her hazel eyes toward Evie. "In three days, you'll be crying because things didn't work out, and two days after that, you'll be hot on another guy's trail."

Evie frowned. "That's not true—"

"It's been true for nearly four years."

That stopped Evie, but Becca continued, "I've seen you through every guy you've dated in college. It's always the same. You're up, then down, then up again, and I'm dizzy from the rollercoaster."

"Becca—"

"Besides, Devon is a womanizer; everyone knows that. What you see in him is beyond me, except for the obvious." Becca shook her head. "I'll see you tomorrow morning if you get in after I'm asleep." She turned the doorknob and left the dorm room.

Evie stared at the closed door, not exactly sure what had just happened. Her roommate had never acted that way before. They'd always talked about their dates, oohing and aahing over which guys they liked. Well, except for the past six months—Becca hadn't been dating much because she was in some pretty intense pre-med classes.

Evie had changed her major more than once, and finally, in her junior year, she'd decided on graphic design in journalism. Two months until graduation, and she hadn't gotten a job offer at a major newspaper yet. One offer had come from a small-town weekly newspaper, but it would only be part-time at the most. And Evie was done with small towns.

She'd absolutely loved living in San Antonio the past four years and attending college. Which meant she went home as little as possible to her small-town roots in Prosper. She loved her family, but she never had any close friends in school. Besides, Evie was a city girl. Her mom wanted her to come back home and work for the *Prosper Weekly.* They didn't even have an online presence.

No, thank you.

Evie refocused on her closet, and true to Becca's prediction, when she walked out of her dorm fifty-five minutes later, she had gone through her entire wardrobe. Becca's as well.

But now, Evie couldn't think about her annoyed roommate, and whether she was in fact on a rollercoaster of dating. As she walked to the commons, where she'd be meeting Devon, she thought back to the past few semesters.

Leaving her small town of Prosper and entering college in the larger city of San Antonio, there had seemed to be *so* many guys in college. At first, Evie had been overwhelmed because they looked at her. Talked to her. Paid attention. Asked her out. With her brothers no longer hovering around her, Evie had started accepting dates.

Back home, her one and only date had been her senior prom. That had been a disaster, with Aaron trying to end the night with a kiss on her front porch. Her brother had opened the door before any kiss could happen, and Aaron had taken off.

That had been the beginning of her almost-kisses that never panned out. Because, well, there was one thing that Evie had never told anyone. Not even her best friend.

Evie still hadn't been kissed.

Yeah, stop the presses, or whatever. Everyone had a dark secret, right? On the outside, it might look like Evie was a flirty girl who dated a lot. Was in it just for fun. Nothing ever serious. But in truth, after three dates, sometimes four, she ghosted the guy. Because that's when the expectations started.

First dates were always flirty, getting-to-know-you. *Where are you from? Do you have siblings? What are you doing after college?*

Second dates were more amped up. *We like each other enough to hang out again, so something more needs to happen.* Like holding hands. Small touches. *How many boyfriends have you had? When did you last have a girlfriend? How long did it last?* A hug good night at the end of the evening.

Third dates were when the expectations skyrocketed. Holding hands again. More touching. And a stolen kiss, or two. Sometimes heading into something much more, if Evie was to base her knowledge on the countless dating stories she'd heard from friends, including Becca.

When Becca asked Evie if she'd kissed her date, she'd say "yes," then change the subject. Because telling the truth, and saying no, that she'd never been kissed, wasn't something Evie wanted to analyze. Well, okay, she'd analyzed it to death, but she didn't want anyone else jumping into her head.

It was bad luck, she'd decided. Unattainable, undefinable bad luck. Every time she'd been about to be kissed, something had happened. Some sort of interruption. Once, it was lightning. Seriously.

"Hi, Evie," someone said, and she looked up to see a woman who'd been in some of her classes.

"Hey, Rachel."

Rachel smiled and continued walking, and Evie realized she was nearly to the commons—the hangout place at the university. Tonight was no different. Students perched on tables and sat on benches. Some were eating ice cream from the university creamery. Beyond was a green belt, and a grass volleyball game was in full swing under the park lights.

Evie scanned the far north table, where Devon had said he'd meet her. Right now, another couple was there, holding hands, and looking like they weren't going anywhere anytime soon.

Evie blew out a breath as she headed toward the table. She couldn't kick them off, so she'd just stay close in order to see Devon when he crossed the commons. She knew which direction he'd come from: the football house, where a bunch of the players lived.

The football house was a huge party destination from what she'd heard. Evie had stuck to the dorms after hearing nightmare stories of girls not paying their share of utilities or having all-night ragers. Just because Evie hadn't been kissed yet didn't mean that she was anti-partying or having fun. But she loved her sleep, and her grades were important. She came from a hard-working ranch family, and money might not be exactly tight, but Evie didn't want to take advantage of her parents agreeing to cover her living expenses so she could take full-time classes.

Her summer jobs helped with the expenses as well, and she'd also stored up some savings in case she didn't get employed right away.

"Are you waiting for someone?" a low voice said next to her ear.

Evie nearly jumped out of her skin. She turned around, pretty sure she was fully blushing. And there he was. Devon. The hottest guy on campus. His blonde hair was teased into messy spikes, and his dark green eyes were fringed with long eyelashes that should be illegal. But it was his smile that tugged at every woman's heartstrings on campus.

That smile was directed at her right now, and Evie's face flamed. Because at that moment, Devon grasped her hand and said, "Wanna go to a party?"

2

CARSON HUNT SLAPPED HANDS and bumped fists as he walked through the football house. The party was under way, and half the team had already shown up, in addition to the five guys who lived there. Plenty of women had arrived, all looking the same, in Carson's opinion. Short skirts, tight tops, layers of makeup. And they were all after one thing. Football players.

The music thumped, the big screen TV blared, and pizza covered the kitchen table and most other surfaces in the front room.

"What's up, Carson?" said Baker, a burly lineman who was already getting interest from pro scouts. "Decided to hang with the dogs, tonight?"

Carson laughed as he paused in the kitchen. "I'm only here for a minute. Have you seen Devon?"

Baker made a show of looking around, then he swung his gaze back to Carson. "Nope. But I'm sure he'll show up with a chick on his arm."

Carson nodded as if it was no big deal to wait for Devon, but inside, he was seething. Devon might be a great quarterback, but he wasn't infallible. Carson was the TA for Devon's biology class, and today, he'd been grading papers. Devon's paper from earlier in the semester was its usual hack job, but the most recent one was excellent.

Carson was positive Devon hadn't written it. But before talking to the professor, or the football coach, Carson wanted to have a one-on-one.

"There he is," Baker said.

But Carson didn't need to be told, because the front room erupted into cheers and welcomes as Devon stepped in. Even though it was early March and off-season for football, Devon was still a hero everywhere he went. Such was the power of football in Texas.

Carson leaned against the counter as he watched Devon weave through the people, stopping and slapping backs, laughing, and sometimes introducing the woman at his side. She wasn't his usual type of date, and that made Carson curious, but he wasn't here to check out women.

Regardless, he eyed her. She wore a blue summer dress that reached her knees, and her dark blond hair fell in waves down her back. Carson guessed it reached nearly to her waist when it was straight. And she seemed keyed up, as if she were nervous or uncomfortable. Her lips were a pale pink, and her makeup muted, making her look a lot younger than she probably was.

Devon grabbed two beers and handed one to the woman, but she shook her head.

Huh. Interesting. A college girl who didn't drink? Especially one with Devon?

Devon was almost to the kitchen, and Carson planned to corner him and demand answers. Carson might have played his four years at another university and transferred here for the master's program, but he was loyal through and through to the football program. He knew the work that went into running a college sports program, and he wouldn't let Devon stain the reputation of the school, no matter how good of a player he was.

Instead of coming into the kitchen, Devon veered to the right, toward the staircase. He was taking his date upstairs.

Not on Carson's watch. But by the time he made it through the crowd to the base of the stairs, Devon and his date had already disappeared. Wow, the guy worked fast. And the woman with him? Apparently, she didn't mind, either.

Well, Carson was about to crash a party of two. He bounded up the stairs and followed the hallway to Devon's bedroom. The guy had a different woman every week—the rumors had even reached Carson—but why should that bother him? Maybe it was because Devon's date didn't look like she'd ever been to a frat party in her life.

The bedroom door wasn't even closed, and Devon was leaning into his date, his hand on her hip. But she wasn't cozying up to him; in fact, she looked like a deer staring into a pair of headlights.

"Devon," Carson said.

Devon's grin was lazy when he turned his head slowly. "Carson. Glad you could make the party, but I'm busy here."

Before Carson could say one word of explanation, Devon swung the door shut in his face.

The click of the lock sent a shot of disbelief through Carson. At first, he only stared at the door, stunned into silence.

Then he heard the woman inside say, "Maybe we should go downstairs."

Devon chuckled. "But I want you to myself."

"No, Devon. I don't think—"

It took Carson only two seconds to open the door with a bit of force from his shoulder. The lock would have to be replaced, but that wasn't his problem.

Both Devon and his date turned, and Carson grimaced at what he saw. The woman had pulled away from Devon, but his large hand held her wrist.

"Let go of her," Carson ground out.

Devon's eyes blazed. "Get the hell out of my room, Carson. None of this is your business."

"She said *no*," Carson said. "Look at her. She looks like she's going to puke, and she hasn't even had a beer."

Devon's gaze swung to his date, and she wrenched out of his grasp.

Before either guy could say anything, she fled the room. Carson had guessed right. The woman had wanted to back-pedal the second Devon brought her to the party.

But now Carson had an angry quarterback on his hands. Not that anyone could intimidate Carson, who had a good two inches on the guy. And although he hadn't played football for nearly two years, Carson hadn't slacked off on conditioning.

And it only took another two seconds to slam Devon against the wall. "First of all," Carson growled, "whoever that chick was, I hope she steers clear of you. And second of all, you're about three minutes away from getting expelled from school."

Devon's eyes popped wide.

"That's right," Carson said. "Consider this a courtesy visit. I expect you to show up Monday morning in Dr. Purcell's office with a full confession."

"I don't know what you're talking about—"

Carson shoved harder, and Devon clamped his mouth closed.

"Good boy." Carson scowled. "Now, I suggest you get this pigsty cleaned up. Oh, and you might want to tell your friends to go home. I think someone has called the cops, and I have no doubt there's a few underage drinkers downstairs."

As if to emphasize Carson's words, a drunk couple stumbled into the room, lips locked.

"Get out," Carson ground out.

The couple stumbled out of the room.

Carson was done. He'd gotten his message across, and now the next move would be Devon's, and hopefully, he'd do the right thing. Carson headed out of the bedroom and down the hall, and by the time he reached the bottom of the stairs, his mind was on the woman again—the one who'd taken off.

He could only hope she'd stay away from Devon from here on out. Why Carson was worried about one of Devon's fans, he had no idea.

He headed out into the cool spring night. San Antonio was usually warmer in March, but the weather had been cool this week. He strode away from the football house and its lights and laughter and shouting. He'd once been one of those guys, having fun all the time, but that had changed his junior year on the football team. His older brother, Rhett, had died in a motorcycle accident, and Carson's world had been rocked.

He'd gone home for the funeral, and when he'd returned to school, it was all he could do to keep his head above water. School, practice, games. That was it. He had no emotional strength left for his then-girlfriend or any of his other friends. Yeah, Stacee had eventually dumped him, and his friends outside of the football team had faded off.

But life went on. He was about to graduate in a couple of months with a master's, then he'd be taking over his grandad's business.

Carson squinted against the series of street lamps when a familiar figure came into view up ahead. Well, a familiar dress, to be exact. It wasn't like he'd forget that blue summer dress in just a few minutes. Or the woman with the long waves of hair.

11

Where was she going? And didn't she have a car?

Maybe she lived in the dorms that were across campus, which would explain why she was walking. Did that mean she was a freshman? Carson was nearly to his truck when he saw the woman stop, then spin around.

She set her hands on her hips and said, "Are you following me?"

Carson halted, stunned. She could only be talking to him. "Um, no. My truck's right there."

Her gaze shifted to the midpoint between them, where, sure enough, his white truck was parked. About ten years old, it had seen better days, but Carson kept it in good shape.

The woman folded her arms now. "What are you, a cowboy or something?"

He frowned. Her tone had been full of animosity. "Got something against cowboys, sweetness?"

She groaned. "You *are* a cowboy." She shook her head like she was truly annoyed with him, then turned and began to walk again.

Carson had no idea what had just happened.

He continued on to his truck and had unlocked it when he realized she'd stopped again. She was watching him, and he felt her hesitation coming off of her in waves, even though they were standing about twenty feet apart.

He didn't know why she'd stopped or why she was currently staring at him, but he felt compelled to ask, "Are you okay?"

When she said nothing, he continued, "Did Devon . . . hurt you?"

She exhaled. "No. I mean, I think he was just going to kiss me."

Carson knew Devon was after more than a kiss.

"And that would have really sucked," she said.

Well, Carson agreed, but he still had a question. "Why were you with him?"

Another exhale. "I thought he was cool. And when he asked me out, I was excited, I guess. I didn't think he'd take me to a raging party, and then, well, you know."

Carson did know. And she'd walked a few steps closer to him. He studied her in the lamp light. "You don't seem his type in the first place. Besides, he can be a jerk, despite his football god status."

The woman looked down at the sidewalk. "Thanks for, um, interrupting things. I didn't realize Devon would take me to his bedroom on our first date."

Carson decided this woman was too naïve for her own good.

"I should go," she said in a rush. "Thanks again."

Carson still hadn't come up with a response as he watched her hurry away, and she'd disappeared around the next corner before he could ask her if she wanted a ride.

3

"YOU'RE BACK EARLY," BECCA SAID, curiosity pushing through her voice.

Nodding, Evie shut and relocked the door, then moved to her closet. She quickly changed into a tank shirt and cut-off sweats, then sank onto her bed. As luck would have it—although this time it seemed to be *good* luck—her almost first kiss was interrupted by a guy breaking down a door. Evie had been grateful. Devon had been taking things to the next level extremely fast, bypassing all the standard rules of dates one and two.

Becca looked up from her laptop and lifted her brows. "That fun, huh?"

"Devon is a womanizing jerk."

Becca merely smirked as she refastened the ponytail holding back her red hair. "And you just figured that out?"

"I think I got starstruck, or something," Evie said. "I mean, he's such a good football player and really cute . . ." Her voice trailed off when she saw Becca rolling her eyes.

"What?" Evie said.

"Everyone knows he dates a different girl every week," Becca said. "Be smarter, Evie."

The words stung, but she and Becca went way back, so Evie knew they were said out of true friendship. She pulled a pillow against her chest. "I'm planning on it."

Becca didn't miss a thing. "What happened?" she asked, her tone concerned now.

Evie met her roommate's gaze. "I . . . I'm not exactly sure. It was all so fast and—"

Becca was off her bed in an instant. She sat next to Evie. "What did Devon do?"

"It's not what you're thinking." Evie told Becca all of it. Walking into the party, everyone's eyes on her, going upstairs to his bedroom, how he almost kissed her, and that friend who practically pushed down the door and allowed her to leave.

Becca stared at her, wide-eyed. "Are you sure you're okay?"

"Yeah." Evie swallowed. "Just feeling really dumb, especially because . . ." She should tell Becca; she was her best friend, after all. "I've never been kissed, and Devon was almost my first."

Becca blinked, and Evie fully expected her to laugh, or to shout, "No way!" But neither of those things happened.

Instead, Becca said, "That really explains a lot."

"What do you mean?" Evie asked.

"You never go out with a guy more than a couple of times," Becca said. "At least not enough to get to the kissing stage."

"Is something wrong with me?" Evie asked, leaning against the wall. "It's like I'm crazy about a guy, but when he starts liking me, I imagine my brothers giving him the riot act. And I can't get away fast enough."

Becca leaned against the wall, too. "You just haven't found the right guy yet. You know, a guy you can like beyond a crush."

"I'm going to swear off football players."

Becca laughed. "You'll have no one left to date, then. You swore off basketball players when Ryan stood you up, you swore off soccer players because Braden would never pay his share of the food bill, you swore off musicians because Jim smoked, you swore off political science majors because all they do is argue, you swore off cowboys because you don't want to live in a small town, you swore off accounting majors because they're too boring—"

"Okay, okay," Evie said with a groan. "I get it. There are no guys left for me."

Becca tilted her head. "Why are you so determined to find Mr. Right at college? I mean, we're only twenty-two and have our whole lives ahead of us."

Evie closed her eyes, because she didn't really want to answer the question. It was selfish of her, but this whole night had proved to her that she needed to be smarter, just like Becca had said.

"My mom wants me to return to Prosper after I graduate," she finally said, opening her eyes. "Not just for a vacation, but to live and work. She's already been talking to the owner of the little, tiny Prosper newspaper." She looked down at the pillow in her lap. "I guess I thought if I was in a serious relationship, I could stay here and get a job. Then move with my fiancé, or husband, or whatever he would be."

Becca didn't move for a moment, then she said, "That seems like a lot of work on your part when you could just tell your mom that you don't want to move back home."

Becca had a point—she always had a point—but . . . "You don't know my mom."

"Um, I do know your mom," Becca said. "Tell her, Evie. Going out with Devon was the bottom of the barrel, even for you."

17

Evie knew it, but she didn't want to admit it. "I'm swearing off all guys until I graduate and figure out what I'm going to do with my life. Maybe then, my luck will change."

"Your luck is fine," Becca said, but Evie heard the humor in her voice. "But good for you. It's about time you made a definitive decision."

Evie knew it was easier said than done, and she'd need all the help she could get. So the next morning, she got up the same time as Becca and went to the library with her.

"You're really taking your vow seriously?" Becca said as she tossed her banana peel into the trash can before entering the library.

"I am," Evie said. She probably needed caffeine later.

They settled at an empty table; in fact, most of the library was empty this time of the morning.

"Dang," Becca muttered, gazing at her laptop.

"What?"

"Nothing from my medical school application yet."

"When are you supposed to know?" Evie asked.

"Any day now," Becca said. "Two people in one of my classes already heard back."

Evie nodded. "I'm sure you'll get in. You have, like, perfect grades."

Becca leaned her head on her hand as she continued to scroll through something on her laptop.

Evie opened up her laptop, and instead of starting to work on a research paper, she browsed the website of the main San Antonio newspaper. She wrote down notes about the design and ideas of how to make it more streamlined. Working for a major newspaper would be amazing.

Growing up in Prosper had been fine, but she didn't want to live her adult life in a place where the only social thing to do on the weekend was watch cowboys at rodeo practice.

There wasn't even a movie theater in Prosper. One bar called Racoons, and Evie wouldn't be caught dead in there. Besides, if one of the local boys asked her to dance, one of her brothers would be there to scare him off. With three older brothers, any guy who attempted to ask Evie out in her high school days in Prosper got the third degree.

Her mind shifted back to the party from the night before. She'd hoped that Devon would have taken her on a real date, but his true character had showed up at that party. She should have refused to go into his bedroom, but it wasn't like he'd shut the door or anything, until that other guy had showed up.

She was pretty sure he was a football player, too, even though she hadn't recognized him. He was opposite in looks from Devon. The mystery guy had dark hair, and nearly black eyes. He was taller and broader than Devon, which was a feat. And he'd never answered her question about being a cowboy, although his beat-up truck was a good indication. But it didn't matter, because at the top of her list was not dating any cowboy. She was done with small-town living.

"Oh, wow," Becca whispered. "That guy is here every morning at the library. If I hadn't known better, I'd think he was following me."

Evie glanced up. And froze. A dark-haired guy sat about three tables away, his profile to them. Even though last night she hadn't gotten much of a view of the mystery man in the rushed encounter in the football house, then a conversation outside in the dark, she knew this guy was *him.*

"Evie?" Becca asked. "Are you okay?"

Evie exhaled. "That's him. The guy who threatened Devon."

Becca's brows shot up. "Really? Huh. He looks too old to be a football player."

"You think so?" Evie frowned. She did see what Becca

was talking about, but maybe it was because of the scruff along his jaw and how his personality seemed kind of intense, more serious, no nonsense.

And then, at that exact moment, when both roommates were gawking at the mystery man, he looked over at them.

Evie stifled a gasp and looked down at her laptop, pretending to be absorbed in the screen. She had no idea what Becca was doing, but Evie didn't want to be caught staring. Yet . . . she could feel his gaze on her. Not that she could prove it. But her face had heated, so maybe that could count as proof?

"Oh my gosh," Becca hissed. "He's coming over here."

Evie couldn't move. She wasn't sure if she was breathing, either. Maybe he was walking to the drinking fountain? Or looking for a book? Or . . .

"Hey."

Evie had to look up.

"Hi," Becca said. "Do we know you?"

The guy glanced at Becca, but then his gaze refocused on Evie.

Oh boy. She'd maybe noticed he was good-looking and hunky before, but now . . . in the light of day—or the fluorescents of the library—mystery guy was beautiful. From the slight wave of his dark hair to the depth of his deep brown eyes to the strong cut of his jaw . . . And yep, the stubble along his jaw only heightened the effect. His dark gray T-shirt and well-fitting jeans made no secret that this guy was in top physical shape. And . . . he was wearing cowboy boots. Okay, then. Still, if there was a photo in the dictionary for tall, dark, and handsome, this was it.

He's a cowboy. And a football player. No, thank you. Besides, I made a vow.

"Oh, I know you," Becca blurted in a perfectly normal, cheery tone.

Evie was impressed.

"You're Carson Hunt."

The mystery guy's eyes narrowed just a fraction. Barely noticeable, except to Evie, because she was apparently staring at him.

"I didn't know you transferred here," Becca continued. "Are you a senior or something?"

"I'm done playing ball," he said. "I'm doing my master's here."

"Oh wow," Becca said. "Nice. What's your master's in?"

His gaze had returned to Evie. "Business. Standard MBA."

Evie opened her mouth. Should she say something? Thank him again for his help last night? Nope. No words were coming. She closed her mouth.

"That's great," Becca continued. "Didn't want to keep playing and go pro?"

Those dark eyes narrowed a fraction again. "No. Sports was just a way to pay for school."

Evie should stop staring at him and noticing things like the scrapes on his knuckles—was that from last night? And the way his jaw had flexed at Becca's questions. And how his voice was a step above gravel.

She gazed at her laptop screen, seeing nothing, comprehending none of the words.

"You okay this morning?" he asked.

Becca didn't answer, confirming that Carson Hunt was asking Evie if she was okay. Slowly, she lifted her gaze. "Yeah, I'm fine."

His nod was slight, but his gaze didn't move from hers, not even when Becca started asking questions again.

"Where you from?" Becca said. "It's been a while since I've read your profile."

"I grew up mostly in Dallas," he said. "Where are you from?" Finally, he was looking at Becca, giving Evie a breather.

"Why, I'm from here," Becca said. "Evie and I were assigned to be freshman roommates, and we've stuck together ever since."

"Evie, huh?" he rumbled.

"Yep, and I'm Becca," she said cheerfully. "Nice to meet you, Carson."

He nodded, but then he was looking at Evie again.

She should really say something more than "I'm fine," but Becca seemed to be handling the entire conversation.

"And where are you from, Evie?"

"Uh, I'm, um . . ."

Becca laughed.

She wasn't helping, at all.

"A small town south of here," Evie said. "Probably never heard of it."

Carson folded his arms, drawing Evie's attention to his sculpted arms. Had she already mentioned his dictionary-defined physique?

"She's from Prosper," Becca said. "A teeny, tiny town, but it's famous for the best rodeo for miles."

Carson's forehead creased. "Is that right? Prosper?"

"Her daddy's the mayor," Becca continued. "And her brother's a rodeo star. Rides pro for . . ."

Evie was no longer listening to Becca, because something had shifted in Carson's gaze. Something she couldn't define. It was as if he was . . . amused. The broody, intense look was gone, replaced by a quirk of his mouth. Was something funny?

"Rex Prosper is your dad?" Carson asked.

Wait. What? "Yeah," she managed to say.

Carson slowly shook his head. "That's a coincidence. Looks like we're gonna be neighbors, sweetness."

4

OF ALL THE WOMEN TO walk into the library . . . Sure, Carson had seen the redhead there a few times. But when he looked over at the table with two women, he almost couldn't believe what he was seeing. What were the chances of running into the same woman from the football party?

He'd recognized her immediately, even though her hair was pulled back into a ponytail, and she was wearing a white T-shirt and not her blue dress. In the lights of the library, he saw that her eyes were a lighter blue than he'd thought, and she had a few faint freckles on her cheeks.

Carson was having trouble looking away from Evie's open blue gaze and answering Becca's questions. Maybe he should just hand over his resume to her, for all the questions she was asking. He wanted to keep studying Evie, and figure out why he was so intrigued. Yeah, he'd helped her last night, but that wasn't it. He couldn't understand why she'd be with a guy like Devon.

And what were the chances that she was from Prosper, the very place where his granddaddy had bought the rodeo grounds? A couple of years ago, Grandad had become an investor, but when the Prosper family hit some financial trouble last fall, he bought the rest of the shares. Now he owned it, along with the homestead property adjacent, ironically enough, to Prosperity Ranch.

Oh, Carson had heard all about the town and the ranches. He just hadn't gone to visit yet. Which was changing this weekend with the start of spring break. He'd promised his grandad that he'd check out the new holdings, and decide once and for all if he was willing to take the helm of Hunt and Sons. Grandad had started the company back in the sixties when a big oil company came in and bought all his land. It was an offer no one could refuse. So Grandad made it his mission to invest in small-town rodeos. He was a generous investor and gave plenty of advice on renovations. Now, Grandad wanted to put down roots and retire. And he'd chosen Prosper to do it.

But with Carson's brother's death, there were no "sons" in the Hunt and Sons scenario. Carson's dad had taken off years ago when Carson was thirteen. Grandad had raised him ever since. So yeah, Carson owed the old man a lot. Everything, really. But true to Grandad's classiness, he was letting Carson make the decision, one hundred percent pressure free. At least in theory.

There was plenty of pressure to take over Hunt and Sons, but Carson had promised himself he'd stay open-minded, and that would start this coming weekend with his visit to Prosper. From everything he'd read about Prosper, the rodeo was the main draw, and when there wasn't a rodeo going, the place was real quiet.

That appealed to Carson more and more, the older he became. Here at this college, some recognized him from his football-playing days. But mostly, he was left alone. Back at his alma mater, he'd never had a moment's peace. That is, until his brother died, and he shut himself off from all parties and social events.

"Tell me about Prosper," Carson said, pulling out a chair and sitting across from the two women.

He saw the surprise on Evie's face, and he also saw the blush on her cheeks. He wasn't sure how to read that since last night, she'd been with Devon. Was she one of those women who fangirled over every athlete? Now that she knew he'd played football, would that impress her?

"Um . . ." Evie looked down at her laptop, her brow creasing.

"She's not a big fan of Prosper," Becca said with a laugh. "Sorry, I can't stay. I've got to get going."

Evie looked at her roommate. "Wait, where are you going?"

Becca merely smiled. "Bye. And nice to meet you, Carson Hunt."

He nodded. "Likewise."

Becca strode off, a smirk painting her face.

Evie watched her friend leave, and then she turned back to her laptop and shut it down.

He sensed she was about to bail as well. "You really hate Prosper that much? Won't even talk about it?"

"It's not that," Evie said, still not looking at him. "I mean, Prosper is great if you like small-town living. But . . ."

He waited. Finally, she met his gaze. Her blue eyes seemed to be troubled, and he didn't like that.

"Let's just say that growing up there, I felt like everything was planned out for me," she said. "I was the mayor's daughter, and with three older brothers, I never got to be myself. Or even figure out who I was. It was like my life had been planned since birth."

"What kind of plan?" Carson asked. This was not the answer he was expecting, but he was definitely intrigued.

"Oh, you know," Evie said, running her hand over her

ponytail. "Marry a local boy, raise babies, Sunday dinner at my parents', working the ranch or chasing kids from sunup to sundown, and then it would start all over the next day."

Carson nodded. "Some would call that an ideal life."

Evie's cheeks pinked. "Right. And I don't know why I'm telling you all this. I know I sound spoiled and selfish, but I've never felt that Prosper was my home. It's always been my family's home, but not *mine*." She shrugged and slipped her laptop into her backpack. "I mean, you'll probably love it."

"Why do you say that?"

She waved a hand in his direction. "You're like the perfect cowboy type."

Carson smiled. "I'm *what*?"

"You know," she said in a rush. "You're all strong and sturdy, and you can probably rope steers on the first try."

"Who said I was a cowboy?"

Her eyes widened. "Um, well, your beat-up truck, for one. And," she scooted her chair back and peeked under the table, "those scuffed-up boots of yours. They're not for decoration."

When her gaze met his again, she found that he was grinning. "You're a smart woman, Evie Prosper." He stood because she stood. "But you got one thing wrong."

Her brow quirked. "Like what?"

"No one's perfect, ma'am."

She rolled her eyes, which made Carson laugh. But there was no smile from her, only a final glance cast at him before she strode out of the library. He folded his arms and watched her go. He guessed her to be about five-eight, and those black jeans of hers made her look even taller. At six-three himself, he appreciated a taller woman.

What was he thinking? Becoming interested in a woman right now wasn't a good idea. He didn't know where he'd be in a couple of months. And if he did end up at Prosper as a home base, it was clear that Evie Prosper wouldn't be there.

Not that he was thinking of her in that way . . . seeing her again had just been a coincidence. One that wouldn't happen again. Unless she was going home for spring break?

He had no time to wonder such things. He needed to get to Dr. Purcell's office. He wanted to be there when Devon walked in the door, if only as a reminder that Carson knew the truth, and Devon had better man up.

But when he got to the biology department, Devon was already leaving the office.

"How'd it go?" Carson asked, expecting him to slow down, be civil. Maybe even apologize.

But that's not what happened.

"Stay out of my business, Hunt," Devon spat as he kept walking down the hall. Within seconds, he was out the door, leaving Carson to stare after him.

Well, then.

Carson shook his head and continued to Dr. Purcell's office. He found the professor sitting at his desk, leafing through a booklet.

"You're here," Dr. Purcell said, lifting his head. His thick brows nearly touched in the center, and his dark gray eyes could be intense, just like now.

"What did Devon say?" Carson asked, leaning against the doorframe.

"I assume you put him up to the meeting?"

"I did." Carson explained what he suspected and how he'd visited Devon the night before. He left out the door-bashing and the near choke hold, but he was sure that Dr. Purcell understood the fuller picture.

"Well, our meeting was technically confidential," Purcell said, his gray eyes narrowing. "But for your information, Devon denies cheating."

Carson scrubbed a hand through his hair. "Really?"

"But . . ." Purcell hesitated. "Let's just say he got the fear of God put into him." The edge of his mouth lifted. "I went down the list of all he could lose, now and in the future. I think you're going to see a different style of paper in his final project."

Carson wanted to slam a fist into the doorframe. Devon was such a punk. If he'd just owned up to his cheating ways . . . There would be some discipline, yeah, but Devon could rise above it and reform.

"So we're back to square one with Devon?" Carson asked.

"I hope not," Dr. Purcell said. "He knows what we suspect, and that might possibly be enough."

Carson gave a curt nod. "All right, then." He paused. "I'm leaving early on Saturday, but I'll get any grading done over spring break that's needed."

"Ah, going home for the week?"

"Not exactly," Carson said. "I'm going to check out a place that might be my future job."

Dr. Purcell nodded. "Great. If you change your mind about needing a letter of reference, let me know."

"I will." Carson left the professor's office then. Devon's actions were frustrating to say the least. That pompous—

"Hey, Hunt," someone said, and Carson looked up.

"Hi, Brad." The kid was in the biology class that Carson was the TA for. Brad was smart, and he'd definitely have a future in the medical field if he chose to pursue it.

The two passed each other, and Carson continued to the empty classroom. He'd spend the next hour doing research on a case study for one of his group projects with the MBA program. He was in charge of the financial analysis that would tie in the recommendations his group would give about restructuring an athletic company. All fictitious, of course, but it was an interesting project. His grandad might enjoy hearing about it.

Carson veered into a short hallway with the drinking fountains in order to fill up his water bottle. He stopped in his tracks when he saw a woman sitting on the bench on the other side of the drinking fountain. He stopped, because it wasn't just any woman. "Evie?"

5

WOW. WHAT WERE THE chances? Again?

Evie straightened from where she'd hunched over her laptop and looked up to see Carson Hunt, of all people. "Are you following me?"

Carson's mouth quirked. Had she noticed before that he had a very nice mouth? Possibly a kissable mouth, not that she'd know or had anyone to compare him to.

"No . . . I'm the TA in one of the biology classes. What are you doing here?"

"Oh." Evie smoothed back her hair; why, she didn't know. It was already in a ponytail. But Carson looming over her made her feel self-conscious. Like she should check her reflection in a mirror or something. And, yeah, seeing him standing there in his cowboys boots, there was no denying he was the type of guy she needed to stay away from. And . . . he was still waiting for an answer, apparently. "This area looked quiet and deserted. So I'm here working on stuff until my next class."

His nod was slow. "Are you taking biology?"

"Oh, heavens no. I did the general class my freshman

year," she said. "Science is not really my thing. But apparently, you're pretty good at it if you're a TA?"

Carson's gaze perused her.

Was she blushing?

"Not exactly," he said. "I mean, I did fine in biology. The TA thing is a paid job."

"Right." Evie should really get back to researching for her paper and stop talking to insanely good-looking former football players and current cowboys. She looked down at her laptop and tapped out a few things. Giving the guy a hint.

He took it. Carson moved to the water fountain and proceeded to fill up a water bottle he'd dug out of his backpack. Evie might have peeked at him once or twice. His dark, wavy hair seemed more mussed up than she remembered. Maybe he'd ran his fingers through it? And by the tenseness of his shoulders, she wondered what he was thinking about.

Whoops. He glanced up and caught her staring.

Her gaze quickly reverted to her laptop.

"You never told me why you're in *this* building," he said, twisting the cap on his water bottle. "I'm here a lot, and I've never seen you here before."

Evie swallowed. "Well, I usually study at the commons, like half the students do. But since my vow, I'm keeping to myself. You know, avoiding distractions."

He was watching her intently. "What vow?"

Had she just told him she'd made a vow? Apparently, she had. She puffed out a breath. "A vow to stay away from idiots like Devon."

Carson's mouth turned up. "Good plan."

When she didn't say anything more, he said, "I feel like there's more to this vow."

Evie really, really liked all this attention from Mr. Hot

TA, but just hanging out with him was sort of against her vow. "There is. But why do you care?"

Her retort didn't even faze him. In fact, he bent and drank some water from the fountain. Then he straightened again. "Like I said, we're going to be neighbors."

At least he hadn't called her *sweetness*, like he had two times before. It was just a Texan endearment, meant very little, but still . . . coming from a guy like Carson Hunt, the butterflies in her stomach had sat up and paid attention. Evie gave the most nonchalant shrug possible. "I don't spend much time in Prosper, but you're welcome to hang out with my brothers."

Carson laughed, and she could swear that his eyes lightened in color. The deep rumble of his laugh stirred up those butterflies again. Evie wanted to press her hand to her stomach to stop them from spinning.

"I'll make a note of that, sweetness." He tipped his hat— an imaginary hat—then strode away.

When he disappeared around the corner, Evie squeezed her eyes shut. It was like the Fates were playing a terrible joke on her. She'd vowed, in good faith, to stay away from attractive men so she'd stop making a fool out of herself. Yet in the farthest corner of the biology department, she wasn't safe.

"Hey, Evie?"

Her eyes flew open, and she turned her head.

Carson was back, hovering near the end of the hallway.

"Yeah?" she said in a faint voice.

"You goin' to Prosper for spring break?"

She inhaled, then exhaled. "I am."

"Then I guess I'll see you there," he said in that low tone of his. "Maybe you can show me around the place."

"Maybe," she said, because she didn't want to commit.

"Do you need a ride?" he asked.

Why was he still here? Still talking to her?

"I have a car," she said, "but thanks."

One of his brows lifted slightly. "If you change your mind, the offer still stands. No use wasting gas if we're both going the same way."

She blinked a few times. As if. "I won't change my mind."

With another nod, he was gone. Evie waited a few minutes, listening, until she was sure he wasn't coming back. Then she covered her mouth and silently screamed out her frustration.

By the time she returned to her dorm room that afternoon, she was finished with the research for her paper. See what a bit of focus and hiding out from all things male had accomplished?

Becca wasn't back yet, which was fine. Evie wouldn't get bored. She could peruse social media as a bit of a break, then she'd start on outlining her paper. She turned her phone back on since she'd turned it off in her last class. Several alerts chimed, telling her that both her mom and dad had left voicemails.

The hairs on the back of her neck stood, because with her mom being a cancer survivor, a phone call from both parents might not bode well. She listened to her dad's first.

"Hey, sweet pea, I wanted to check on your travel plans this weekend. Holt said the last time he was up there and visited, he thought your car might need some maintenance. So that needs to be taken care of, unless you want to take the bus."

Evie wouldn't be taking the bus. She did that over Christmas break and ended up catching a head cold from one of the passengers who kept coughing. Not that she was a huge germaphobe, but public transportation was sketchy.

Next, she listened to her mom's voicemail.

"Sweetie, I'm wondering if you can get one of those university sweatshirts in a kid size. Holt's got Ruby all worked up that you're coming home for spring break, and I think it would be a nice gift. I can transfer the amount to your account."

Evie deleted both voicemails, then called her mom.

"Is this a prank call?" her mom answered with a laugh.

Okay, so Evie was terrible at returning phone calls. "No, I got your message. And I can get that sweatshirt. What size is she?"

"I don't know," her mom said, a smile in her voice. "Little girl size?"

"Right." Ruby was Evie's niece, and she was adorable. Had the whole family wrapped around her little finger, especially Evie's dad.

"Did you hear about Cara?" her mom continued.

Evie refrained from rolling her eyes. Her younger sister was on a full-ride scholarship to a top culinary school in Texas, and she'd been awarded an internship in Dallas with some fancy chef. It wasn't just that she was getting some recognition at the age of twenty, but it seemed like every time Evie talked to her mom, she had to hear all about how amazing Cara was. "Yeah, I read the email."

"Oh, I wasn't sure, since you never reply to them."

Ouch. "I'm excited for her. When does she start?"

"In April," her mom said. "Although, I think she'll be too busy until then to make it back home."

It was always about *home* for her mom. When one person was coming, and when one person was leaving.

"Did you call her with a congratulations?" her mom said.

"I texted her," Evie said, then winced. Texting was never good enough for her parents. Phone calls were acceptable.

Then emails were number two on the tier. Texting was probably below old-fashioned letter-writing.

Her mom's exhale was faint.

"How are you feeling, Mom?" Evie asked. Her mom had received the six-month bill of health, but that only started the countdown to the next oncology appointment.

"Great, actually," her mom said. "I'm helping Barb out with the 4-H club now."

If a queen could be elected for Prosper, it would be Barb. She ran every committee for every event. She'd been a couple of years older in school than Evie, but she was the reigning queen of the popular girls. "Sounds fun," Evie said, trying to keep any sarcasm out of her tone.

"We can't wait to see you, dear," her mom continued. "What time are you leaving on Friday?"

"Um, first thing in the morning," she said. "Hey, I wondered if the old Anderson place had sold yet?"

Her mom went silent for a heartbeat. "Funny you should ask. It sold right after New Year's."

"Huh, interesting," Evie said, wanting to ask more, but then her mom would set in with the questions. Besides, it wasn't like she'd be hanging out with Carson Hunt, anyway. He could get a tour of the town from someone else. "So it will only be Lane and Holt around during spring break?"

"Yes, Knox is on the rodeo circuit."

Right, her brother who'd shattered his life, and now was trying to pick up the pieces. Hopefully, this time it would work, and he wouldn't fall back on his self-destructive ways.

"Have you given more thought to the *Prosper Weekly*?" her mom continued.

Evie should have expected the question. It had been a question over and over.

"You could meet with Bev Jarvis," her mom said. "I told her you were coming."

Evie already knew that, too. "I'll think about it," she finally said. "I've got my resume several places right now." It was true, but no major newspapers had replied.

Her mother's silence said more than words could have.

Evie hated that she felt like she was disappointing her mother, but she was an adult woman now, and she'd been living away from Prosper for four years already.

"I should go," Evie said. "I'm working on a paper. You can tell Dad that I'm driving. Holt gave me a rundown of things to check on my car, and I'm going to do that before I leave."

"All right, sweetie," her mom said with a small sigh in her voice. "Can't wait to see you. Love you."

"Love you, too." When Evie hung up with her mom, she didn't return to her laptop for a while. What would it be like to work in Prosper? Well, she knew what it would be like. She'd be in a rut, that's what. If she thought dating was hard in college with hundreds of single guys around, Prosper would be impossible.

Maybe she should take her car into the lube and oil place today before they closed. Get a head start on whatever car stuff needed to be done. Then, Evie could refocus on outlining her paper.

By the time she reached the parking lot where her car was, the afternoon had grown late. Evie unlocked her car and climbed in.

She shook away the memory of Carson Hunt offering her a ride to Prosper. He was a presumptuous guy. Starting the car, she shifted into reverse. As she did, something whined. A gear, or something? Whatever it was, it didn't sound good. She shifted into park, then drive. The car shuddered before moving forward. Huh.

Evie bit her lip as she drove slower than normal out of the parking lot. Was the whining sound louder? Was something going to explode on her? She passed a group of students, and by the turn of their heads, she knew they'd noticed the sound, too.

Hopefully, it would be a quick fix so she could leave Friday. But when she pulled into the lube and oil shop, the attendant came out to meet her, already shaking his head.

"You need to take this to the mechanic down the road," he said.

"What do you think is wrong with it?" she asked.

"My guess is that you've got to replace some belts," he said. "We can't do that here."

Evie sighed. "My brother said I needed to get the oil changed before this weekend since I'm driving a couple hundred miles."

The attendant merely shrugged. "Get the belts fixed, then bring it back here. We're open until seven tonight and tomorrow until five. Good luck."

Evie pulled out of the parking lot, wincing at the continued whine. Luckily, the mechanic shop was only a few blocks away. Before she went into the office, she called her oldest brother, Holt. He managed Prosperity Ranch for her dad, and he was less likely to get wound up and worry. His matter-of-fact personality was very much needed right now.

"What's up, sis?" he answered on the third ring.

"Have you ever heard of Johnson's Auto in San Antonio?"

"Uh, not sure," he said. "What's up?"

"My car sounds like a crying baby," Evie said.

Holt chuckled. "Can you be more specific?"

She explained all the sounds and what the attendant at the lube and oil shop had told her. "What if they try to charge me for a bunch of stuff here?"

"Well, you're not driving your car as is," he said. "Go inside and tell them what's going on. When they diagnose it, call me."

"Okay," Evie said, feeling a little better. "Can you talk to them instead?"

"I could . . ." Holt drawled, "but this is a good opportunity for you do this on your own."

"When I get my first real paycheck, I'm going to dump this beast."

Holt laughed. "I bet you will, sis. And I wouldn't blame you. The car has seen better days, but it's important that you be safe. Want me to come and pick you up on Saturday?"

Evie knew if she said yes, her brother would do it. But he was busy keeping the entire family afloat. "No, worst case I'll take the bus."

"Ah." Another laugh from Holt. "We'll never hear the end of that, I'm sure."

She cracked a smile. No, they would not.

6

CARSON TOSSED THE DUFFLE into the bed of his truck. He didn't need much during spring break, and his laptop was snug in his backpack on the truck's bench. He was mostly caught up with school work, but he assumed there'd be some downtime to finish off his part of the group project, plus any grading that might come in from the biology class.

Grandad had already called him twice this morning, and Carson had to smile at that. The old guy was pretty dang excited about his visit. And he could only hope that it would be a win-win for both of them.

Possibly his only regret was that his brother Rhett wasn't here to experience any of these milestones. Not Grandad's recent acquisitions. Not Carson's college graduation. Not this new opportunity in Prosper.

Rhett had been the older brother who'd paved the way for Carson in sports. Carson had been the one to play in college, but Rhett had held his own in high school. He'd also included Carson in all the activities, and it was like he had an automatic friend group the first day of high school.

Sometimes, moments like this, when Carson was transitioning from one thing to another, was when he missed his brother the most. He didn't even want to imagine a time when Grandad would no longer be around. Every time Carson saw him, the guy looked more and more ancient, yet he was the most spunky man alive.

Carson started up his truck and pulled away from the curb. The streets of San Antonio were quiet this early on a Saturday morning. His route leaving the city took him to the bus station.

Carson glanced over at the line of people, a bunch of them probably college students, waiting to get on the bus. A blonde woman caught his attention, and Carson did a double-take. She reminded him of Evie Prosper. But Evie had a car, right? She'd been insistent that she didn't want to carpool with him. Regardless, Carson found himself slowing down and studying the woman in his rearview mirror.

It *was* her. And she was taking a bus? To Prosper?

Carson swerved into the center lane of the road and did a U-turn. He pulled alongside the curb and stopped in front of the bus station.

Yep. Evie Prosper was in the bus line, a backpack slung over her shoulder as she scrolled through something on her phone. Her ratty jeans fit her legs like a second skin, and her pale pink T-shirt almost matched the morning sunrise.

Rolling down the passenger window, he called out, "Evie Prosper!"

She glanced up, her brows lifted. Her mouth formed an O when she saw him, and then something interesting happened. She blushed.

Carson motioned with his hand for her to come toward the truck. He could see her hesitation clear as day, but then she glanced at the bus, and back to him. Soon, she was striding toward him, hitching her backpack on her shoulder.

"You taking the bus home?" Carson asked when she neared.

Evie puffed out a breath. "Yeah. My car's in the shop."

"The offer's still good," he said. "Heading out now, and you'll be home before any bus can get you there."

She bit her lip, glancing back at the bus, then said, "I already bought a ticket, and there's no refunds."

"Tell you what, I won't charge you for gas."

The edge of her mouth lifted, and it was perhaps the first almost-smile he'd seen from her.

"That's mighty gentlemanly of you." She was teasing him, and he knew in that moment, she was going to ride with him.

"I'm happy to oblige, ma'am." He pulled his own back-pack closer to him. "Come on, there's plenty of room. Got a suitcase or anything? The bed's wide open."

"No," she said, reaching for the door handle and popping it open. "I only have my backpack."

He must have looked surprised, because she said, "I might not like living in a small town, but I'm not high maintenance."

"Yes, ma'am," he said, pulling away from the curb the second her door had shut. As he did another U-turn, Evie rolled up her window.

"Thanks for this," she said, her voice quiet.

He glanced over at her. She was holding her backpack in her lap, and her gaze seemed pensive.

"I'm stopping for gas," he said. "Do you need anything, like breakfast?"

Her gaze flitted to his. "I'm not hungry."

He couldn't quite read her, but as he pulled into the gas station, he decided to get her something anyway. It was nearly an hour drive. "There's plenty of room for your backpack on the bench," he said. "Or you can put mine on the floor. But I do insist you wear a seatbelt."

She smirked, and he climbed out of the truck. Once he

had the thing full of gas, he headed into the gas station. He picked up a couple of water bottles, two packaged muffins, a bag of pretzels, and corn nuts, since he wasn't sure what she liked.

Road trip food completed, he returned to the truck. His backpack was still on the seat, and hers was on the floor, but she'd pulled out her laptop. "Homework?"

"Yeah." She furrowed her brow when she saw the stuff he bought.

"Have what you want." He set the sack in the middle of the bench. "I don't want to eat alone."

She scoffed, and then to his surprise, she took one of the muffins out and unwrapped it.

Carson was oddly satisfied that she'd accepted his food offering.

The first part of the drive was quiet, although Carson drummed up question after question in his head. He tried to be respectful of whatever homework she was doing. But it was impossible to ignore the fact that he had a beautiful female passenger in his truck, one he kept stealing glances at. Evie absently played with her hair when she wasn't typing. She'd braided it, and she kept curling the ends around her fingers.

It amused him that she was so fidgety. Had he noticed that before? He hadn't.

"What's your paper on?" he finally asked.

Evie looked up with a start, almost like she'd forgotten he was there.

"Oh, um, I'm researching statistics on newspaper readers switching to online sources."

"Are you majoring in statistics or math?"

"No, graphic journalism."

Carson held her blue gaze for a second. She wasn't wearing any of that fancy eyeliner or lip gloss this morning. He liked it. "Never heard of it."

"I kind of made it up," she said, her lips curving into a smile. "I mean, my major is graphic arts, and my minor is journalism."

Carson glanced at the road, then back to her. "Sounds interesting. What will you do when you graduate?"

"Create graphics for a newspaper website."

"Hmm. Not what I pictured you doing."

She folded her arms. "What did you picture me doing?"

He shrugged. "Maybe a teacher or something. Like at an elementary school."

Evie raised her brows. "Really? Why?"

Well, this conversation had taken a sharp turn. Carson scrubbed a hand through his hair. He needed to tread very, very carefully here. "I don't know you all that well to pass judgment."

She smirked, her blue eyes dancing with amusement. "That's a cop-out, and you know it. Spill it, Hunt."

Hunt, huh? "Okay, I just thought that someone majoring, or minoring, in journalism, would be more . . ." He hesitated.

Her gaze didn't move from his face. "More . . . ?" she prompted.

"You know," he stalled. "More street smart? Someone who would steer clear of guys like Devon. And someone who'd be pestering everyone with questions."

She laughed. The sound caught him off-guard, and then he was smiling, too. "What?"

Evie waved a hand in front of her face as if she were fanning herself. "I'll be staring at a computer all day, not interviewing witnesses to crimes on the street."

"So it's like a computer job?"

"Yeah, mostly," she said. "There will probably be staff meetings where we brainstorm stuff."

"Sounds interesting," he said.

"You sound so convinced."

He shrugged, still smiling. "Maybe you can show me some of the stuff you're working on, so I can get a fuller picture."

She quirked a brow. "Maybe."

The next few miles passed in more silence, then he had to ask, "Okay, so tell me why you're so anti-small town living, and what else did you say? You're opposed to Sunday dinners and raising babies?"

She arched a brow. "You have a good memory, Mr. Hunt."

"Well, thank you, Miss Prosper."

"I'll let you be the judge of Prosper yourself," she said. "My parents love it. My brother Holt is there for good, too."

"Fair enough."

She closed the laptop and slipped it into her backpack. "Finished already?"

Evie shrugged. "I need to save something to do at home."

"Is it really that bad in Prosper?" he asked in a low tone.

She sighed. "It's not that bad; it's just not what I want."

He nodded. "Where do you see yourself in five years?"

"Is that the TA coming out in you? One of the professors rubbed off?"

"Maybe . . ." He glanced at her.

"I don't know where I'll be in five years." She leaned forward and fiddled with the radio. Yeah, there wasn't a CD player or Bluetooth in his truck. Just a radio. "How old is your truck?"

"I was waiting for you to ask that," he said. "It was my grandad's, and he gifted it to me when I got recruited for football." His gaze slid over to her again. She'd crossed those long legs of hers and was currently picking at some threads on one of the ragged holes.

"That was nice of him," she said. "You two must be close?"

"Yeah. He raised me and my brother, Rhett." Before he could say any more, or decide how much he wanted to say in the first place, a car fishtailed in front of them. Carson slammed on the brakes and was able to stop before they became the third car in the chain reaction.

The music was still playing in the cab of the truck, but Carson's thundering heartbeat drowned it out.

"You okay?" he asked, looking over at Evie.

She nodded, but her face was pale. "Yeah. You?" Her hand went to his arm, her fingers cool on his skin.

"I'm fine." He unclipped his seatbelt. "I'll see if anyone needs help. You might need to call 911."

"Okay," Evie said in a barely-there voice.

Carson slid out of the truck and checked on the car that he'd nearly hit. An older couple was inside, and they both looked shaken up. Carson opened the driver's door. "Ma'am, are you all right?"

The woman with thin gray hair rubbed at her neck. "I'm all right."

The older man in the passenger seat had eyes as wide as the moon. "We damn near hit that motorcycle. It just spun out of control in front of us."

Carson's heart sank. He hadn't seen the motorcycle, but motorcycle crashes rarely had a good outcome. He hurried around the spun-out car and jogged to where he could see a human form on the side of the road. His stomach clenched. The person didn't seem to be moving, but at least he was wearing a helmet.

Images flashed through Carson's mind. Images of another motorcycle wreck, one he'd never witnessed but had imagined many times. The guy lying on the side of the road right now could have been Rhett. It *had* been Rhett, and he hadn't survived.

Carson wanted to turn away, turn back time and not be here, in this moment. But what if someone's quick actions had been able to save Rhett's life?

Carson pushed forward, despite the fact that he wanted to puke. He knelt by the inert form and only focused on one thing—not the blood or the possible broken bones—but the man's neck above his collar. Carson placed two fingers on the man's neck to feel his pulse.

He closed his eyes, blocking out all sounds. Voices of other motorists who must have stopped. Someone saying they were calling an ambulance. Carson pressed on the man's skin, trying to concentrate.

Thrum. Thrum. Thrum.

The man's heart was still beating.

Carson opened his eyes as voices drew closer. Someone set a hand on his shoulder. Another person knelt on the other side of the victim and unbuttoned his shirt. "He's alive," a voice proclaimed.

"The ambulance is on its way."

"Young man, can you move back?" another said. "We need to make way for the paramedics."

Was the ambulance already here?

Carson had lost all sense of time and perspective. He moved back, but stayed on his knees.

He couldn't leave until he knew the man was going to be all right. As the EMTs moved in and loaded the man on the stretcher, still Carson didn't move.

Not until someone placed a hand on his shoulder.

"Carson, let's get back in the truck," Evie said, her tone quiet. "The ambulance is leaving."

He should move. But somehow, he was frozen to the spot.

"Carson."

Evie grasped his hand, tugging him upward. Only then did he move to his feet.

Evie wasn't sure how to read Carson. He'd jumped out of the truck and ran to help the fallen motorcyclist. He'd even checked the guy's pulse. And now? Carson's eyes seemed vacant, and he wasn't answering any of her questions. She didn't know a lot of medical stuff, but she wondered if he was in shock or something.

She really should drive, but Carson was climbing into the driver's seat.

When Evie settled into the passenger seat, Carson still hadn't started the truck. Both of his hands were on the wheel as he stared straight ahead.

"Carson?" she said.

He didn't answer her or look at her.

Evie's stomach tightened. Something was wrong, and not just because they'd nearly gotten into an accident. It went deeper than that.

"Carson?" she asked again, then shifted closer to him. His breathing was shallow, and his knuckles white from his tight grip. She placed a hand on his back. That got his attention, and he exhaled.

Evie moved her hand up his back, slowly, then back

down, as if she were giving him a very light back rub. She kept going, because she could see his grip easing on the steering wheel, and his breathing was becoming more normal.

"I think I should drive," she said. "I don't know what's going on right now, but let me help. Please?"

His head slowly turned, and his dark eyes focused on her. "Can you drive a truck?" he rasped.

Evie would have laughed, but she knew this wasn't the time. She'd been driving trucks since she was fourteen. "I can drive a truck," she said. "My dad and brothers made sure of that."

Something like relief crossed his face, and with a nod, he said, "All right. If you don't mind."

He didn't explain what was going on, and she didn't ask. They swapped places, and Evie pulled out onto the road again. Soon, they were going freeway speeds, and Carson seemed to relax more and more as they put the miles behind them. The radio stayed low, and Evie barely paid attention.

Every thought was about Carson, and how he was doing. She glanced over at him, and although he seemed to be in his own world, she felt that whatever tension or anxiety he'd experienced had lessened.

When the sign for the turn-off to Prosper came up, Carson seemed to rouse.

"We're here already?" he asked.

"Yeah," Evie said, glancing over at him. "I can drive you to your grandad's place, then walk to mine. It's not that far."

"I can drive, no worries," Carson said.

His voice did sound stronger, more determined.

"Are you sure?" she asked, not wanting to press, but wanting to be sure. Now that they were finally in Prosper, she found she was breathing easier. Having Carson check out like that had been unexpected.

"Thanks, Evie," he said. "I don't know what happened back there . . ."

"No worries," she said. "Like I said, I'm a pro at driving trucks."

The edge of his mouth lifted as if he wanted to smile, but it was nowhere close to reaching his eyes. "So, where's the hot hangout in town?"

Evie lifted her chin as she turned onto Main Street. "Well, there's the diner if you like a good spicy chili. And the barbershop if you're in need of a trim."

Carson scrubbed a hand through his hair. "That might be a good idea."

No, she wanted to tell him. His hair was perfect how it was. Wow, her brain was taking a hard detour.

"And the ice cream parlor," Evie said. "I mean, it's probably the last standing ice cream parlor for miles around. Everything now is shakes with fast food, or frozen yogurt shops."

"I love ice cream."

Evie smiled and glanced over at Carson. He was looking out the passenger window, and she wondered if he even knew what he'd admitted.

She slowed and stopped at the only traffic light in all of Prosper. As they waited, she pointed to the bar up ahead. "There's Raccoons, the town social center," she said. "At least for those twenty-one and over."

Carson nodded. "The hangout place, huh?"

"For some." Evie pulled forward with the green light.

"Not you?"

She shrugged. She didn't really want the questions, so she didn't elaborate.

"You weren't drinking when you were with Devon," Carson said.

Evie stiffened, wondering how much she should say to him. As far as she knew, they'd get to her place, and she wouldn't see him all week, and possibly ever again. "I don't really drink." She felt his gaze on her. Curious.

"Ever?"

"I've tried it, if that's what you mean," she said. "But it's not for me, I guess. I don't want to be one of those girls who gets sloppy, then regrets stuff or can't remember anything."

Carson didn't answer for a moment, but she could feel his gaze on her. What was he thinking? That she was a prude?

"Good for you," he said at last.

Evie didn't have to be told that. The light changed, and she pulled forward. "Plus, my brothers would kill me if I became a party girl. Even more so than my parents."

Carson's dark brows shot up. "I think I like your brothers."

Evie scoffed, even though she hadn't meant to.

And of course, Carson picked up on it. "What?"

"Believe me, three older brothers is enough to drive a girl crazy," she said. "I only went on one date in high school."

"You're kidding me," Carson said.

"Not kidding." Evie slowed the truck and turned the final corner leading out to Prosperity Ranch. They'd pass by the old Anderson ranch on the way, which was now apparently owned by Carson's grandpa.

"We're almost there," Evie said, if only to effectively change the subject.

"To your place?"

"We'll pass by the old Anderson place on the way—the homestead your grandpa bought."

"Oh, wow." Carson leaned forward in the seat, his eyes intent on the road. "Just drive to your place, then I'll take the truck back."

Fine, that was fine. But . . . what if her family was around? And they met Carson? Evie was already cringing at all the questions that would happen. Of course, they'd be around. They were expecting her to arrive on the bus and text when she got off at the bus stop. But with the delay of the accident, carpooling with Carson had taken about the same amount of time.

She pointed out the turnoff for the old Anderson place, then she took the next road to Prosperity Ranch. Although she'd grown up there, she never failed to appreciate it. The rambler home with a wraparound porch, the circular driveway, and the pristine barn, fields, and small horse arena beyond. Everything was green this time of year.

Carson released a low whistle. "Wow, this place is gorgeous."

A bubble of pride expanded inside of Evie. "Yeah, my dad is kind of a perfectionist, and he passed it onto my brother Holt. He's the manager now."

"They breed horses?" Carson said, obviously noticing the huge barn and the arena just behind it.

"They rehabilitate horses, and they also take on rodeo training," Evie said.

Carson nodded, his gaze full of appreciation as he took in the surroundings.

Evie's heart sank when she saw her dad's truck, her mom's car, and Holt's truck all in the wide circular driveway. And just beyond, another truck that Lane drove. So. Everyone was home.

Evie parked a good distance from the other vehicles. "Thanks for the ride, Carson," she said quickly. "Are you sure I can't give you some gas money?"

Carson swung his gaze to meet hers. "No. I mean you pretty much drove the whole way." His tone lowered. "Thanks for that. I don't know . . ." He sighed.

And just then, the front door opened, and her mom stepped out. She was all dolled up in full makeup, and a yellow blouse and gray slacks. Maybe she'd had a committee meeting today? As she walked to the edge of the porch, she lifted her hand to shade her eyes from the sun.

Evie popped her door before everyone else showed up, but by the time she called hello to her mom and walked around the front of the truck, Holt had come out of the barn.

Holt was her tallest brother, and his brown hair was mostly concealed by his cowboy hat. But his piercing blue eyes took in the scene quickly.

Right. In the quiet countryside, the sound of an approaching truck could be heard by everyone.

And . . . there was Lane, walking from the direction of the arena, her dad right behind him. Lane was a younger version of her mom—blonde hair, blue eyes. And her dad wore his standard outfit of a starched button-down shirt, tan Levi's, polished boots, a black hat, and his leather belt with a buckle that read "Prosperity Ranch."

"I thought you were taking the bus?" her mom said, a question in her tone. She came down the steps and reached the walkway just as Carson climbed out of the passenger seat and shut his door. "Who's this?"

"Mom, this is Carson Hunt," Evie said, then stepped forward and hugged her.

"Oh, hello," her mom said, releasing Evie and extending her hand to Carson.

He shook it, and seconds later, Evie was hugging her brothers and dad in turn, then making the same introduction. She stayed quiet as Carson told them about his grandad and the recent purchase of the adjoining homestead.

"Oh, you're Randy Hunt's grandson?" her dad said.

"Yes, sir."

The two began to talk about the Anderson property—well, mostly her dad was talking, and Carson was listening. All the while, her mom kept glancing at Evie with comical eyes. As if saying, *why didn't you tell me about this guy? Who is he and are you dating?*

All questions Evie was sure would be asked as soon as Carson Hunt got into his truck and drove away.

"Are you two hungry?" her mom said, cutting into the men's conversation, which Lane and Holt had jumped into as well. "I've got some fixings for sandwiches, and I've made a peach pie. From canned peaches, so not as good as my fresh peach pie."

Evie held her breath, wondering what Carson would say. She was both relieved and disappointed when he said, "I should get going. Grandad will be expecting me."

"Sure, sure," her dad said. "Tell him he's welcome here anytime."

"Why don't the two of you come over for dinner tonight?" her mom chimed in. "Six o'clock work?"

Leave it to her mom to make everyone best friends.

"I'll, uh, talk to Grandad," Carson said. "Then I'll let you know, Mrs. Prosper. I appreciate the offer."

Well. This was going to be interesting, because her mom's smile was as wide as the Texan sky. And Holt and Lane were now exclaiming over Carson's old truck as if it were some sort of collector. Which, it wasn't.

But Evie refrained from rolling her eyes.

"It's so good to see you," her mom said, moving closer and wrapping her arm about her waist. "And what a surprise to show up with such a nice young man."

"Mom, hush," Evie hissed. "He's right there."

"Oh, those boys aren't paying us one bit of attention," she said. "Come on inside and see Ruby. I'm watching her for the afternoon, and she's taking a nap, but I need to wake her before she messes up her sleeping schedule."

"Where's Macie?" Evie asked, following her mom inside.

"She had to get some supplies for her bracelets in the next town over."

Macie used to be married to her brother Knox—and Ruby was their kid. But their marriage fell apart, and when Macie brought Ruby for an extended visit last summer at Prosperity Ranch, everyone's world turned upside down.

Because Macie and Holt fell in love.

And now, they were married, happily.

It had been a shock to the whole family, especially her mom, who'd been holding out for a reconciliation for Knox and Macie. But now, even Evie could see that Holt was better suited to Macie.

Her mom stopped at the spare bedroom that was once Cara's bedroom. A small form was under the covers, her brown curls spilling out over the pillow. Ruby was darling when she was asleep, precocious when awake, and everyone in the family hung on her every adorable word.

Evie walked with her mom across the room and watched as she smoothed Ruby's hair from her face.

"Ruby, dear," her mom said in a singsong voice that apparently grandmothers used for their grandchildren. "Time to wake up."

Ruby stirred, and her eyelids fluttered, but she didn't wake.

"Guess who's here?" her mom continued in that sweet tone. "Your Aunt Evie."

Ruby's brown eyes snapped open, and an impish grin spread across her face. "Evie!"

Evie laughed and had to brace herself against the bed as Ruby launched herself into her arms.

"How are you, baby?" Evie asked, squeezing her niece tight. She smelled of oranges and . . . milk?

"I'm not a baby!" Ruby exclaimed, pulling back and patting Evie's cheeks. "I'm four!" Her cheeks were flushed pink from sleep, and her brown curls a wild nest.

"Oh, wow," Evie said. "How did you get so old?"

Ruby wrinkled her nose.

"You must be a real lady now," she continued.

Ruby giggled. Then she wrapped her little arms about Evie's neck in nearly a choke hold. "I missed you," her niece said.

Evie's heart swelled, and warmth flooded to her feet. "I missed you, too, little lady."

8

CARSON FOUND GRANDAD IN the back of the house, with a rake in one hand, a cigarette in the other, and a worn cowboy hat atop his head.

Carson grinned. Grandad hadn't changed, and likely never would. Carson crossed the patches of stubby grass and reached the edge of what must have been a former garden before Grandad noticed him.

"Hey, Grandad," he said.

The old guy started, then looked up from where he'd been frowning at a collection of rotted tomato plants.

"Carson!" he said, his smile wide on his leathery face. The man's brown eyes mirrored his own. "I was wondering when in the Sam you'd get here."

Carson chuckled. When his grandad took over raising Carson and Rhett, he'd curbed his cursing. So instead of saying "Sam hell" he started saying "Sam." The habit had stuck ever since.

"I told you I'd be here by lunchtime."

Grandad perched the rake against his hip, then swept off his hat and scratched at his few wisps of remaining hair, somehow managing not to singe his head with his cigarette.

They weren't really a hugging family, but Grandad's grin was like the strongest hug Carson could ever get.

"So, what? You expecting me to feed you now?" Grandad said with a chortle.

"Do I need to rake this mess of a garden before I earn my food?" Carson teased.

"I think I can scrape something up." Grandad plunked his hat back on. "A boy like you needs something in his belly."

Carson and his brother had always been "boys" to Grandad.

"I have a feeling that I'm going to be doing all the cooking this week," Carson said.

"Yep, you're right." Grandad headed toward the back of the house, which had seen better days—much, much better days. "That's why I taught you to cook, boy. I'm in my payback years. Collecting on all the time I spent on you boys."

Carson clapped a hand on his grandad's bony shoulder. "We'll count today as day one then."

Grandad stomped his boots on the back patio, which needed a good sweeping, then propped the rake against the wall of the house. Carson glanced around before following him into the house. Cracked planters lined the patio, as if someone had once had this place decorated with flowering plants. Beyond the rotted garden was about two acres of field. Edging the property was a brown, splintered fence that served as an ineffective barrier to any horse, or cow.

Carson stepped inside the dim interior of the home.

The place smelled musty, and his first impression was that the whole house probably needed to be gutted. New carpet, new paint, even new counters and cupboards in the kitchen were needed. The musty smell likely came from the well-worn carpet and the threadbare couch and overstuffed chair.

"Come on in, don't be shy," Grandad said, moving about the kitchen after turning on an overhead fluorescent light that washed everything a dull yellow.

Well, the countertops and the linoleum were, in fact, technically yellow.

"Are you thinking of getting any animals?" Carson asked.

"Maybe a horse, but that's all I can care for by myself until you get here," Grandad said. "I've got to get that garden into shape before summer hits and it's too late to grow."

Carson perched on a rickety stool, knowing from experience not to get in Grandad's way when he was in the kitchen. It was either Grandad or Carson who prepared meals, not both together. So he watched Grandad move about, opening cupboards, pulling out two cans of chili, then a box of soda crackers from another cupboard.

Carson thought about the chili Evie had mentioned from the diner on Main Street. He wasn't picky though, especially when he was hungry.

As Grandad warmed up the chili in a cooking pot, he said, "After we eat, I'll give you a tour of the place, then we'll head over to the rodeo. I'll go through my plans for the arena and see what you think. See if you can use that education of yours to give me some pointers as well."

"All right," Carson said. "What about this house? Got any plans to, uh, fix it up?"

Grandad chuckled as he stirred the now bubbling chili. "That's what you're for, boy. You're young and strong and here for a week. Don't be thinking you're going to be taking long naps and watching the telly."

Carson scoffed. "Do you even have a TV?"

Grandad used the wooden spoon he was stirring with to point to the far side of the room, where a wide, flat box was propped against the wall. "Right there, son. And you're gonna install it. Don't think I'm going to live here in the dark ages."

Carson laughed. "You're still hooked on *Law and Order*, aren't you?"

"They've got the reruns on cable," Grandad said. "I already paid for the service; I just need you to hook everything up."

"You know, the cable company can do that for you."

"Not when my boy's coming in town."

Right . . .

"Lunch is ready," Grandad announced, pouring two even bowls of the bubbling chili. Then he proceeded to crush the soda crackers over the top like a garnish.

Carson dug in. It wasn't bad for canned chili, and although he didn't add Tabasco sauce like Grandad did, it hit the spot.

"Oh, hey, I almost forgot. Mrs. Prosper invited us for dinner tonight. I said I'd talk to you first."

Grandad's brow wrinkled. "How did that invitation come about?"

So Carson told him the basics of giving Evie Prosper a ride.

"Evie? I haven't met her. I met the other sister, Cara or something, and she's not your type."

Carson almost choked on his current spoonful of chili. He swallowed and cleared his throat. "I'm not looking for a girlfriend, Grandad."

Grandad set down his spoon, then took a long swig from his water glass. "It's been two years, son. You haven't dated anyone since Stacee."

Carson blinked. Grandad had never mentioned Stacee before, at least not since they broke up after Rhett died. He didn't realize it was something Grandad had been thinking about.

"How do you know I haven't been dating?" Carson asked, feeling a bit defensive.

Grandad's brown eyes had lost all their twinkle. "I know you better than you think, boy. It's in your demeanor when I see you, your tone when we talk on the phone."

"That I'm not *dating*?" Carson said, scrubbing a hand through his hair. "How so?"

Grandad merely grunted, then turned from the counter and rustled for something in the pantry. "Here you go," he said, producing an old, beat-up cowboy hat. The only redeeming quality was that it was in better shape than the one Grandad currently wore. "Got ya something. It'll keep the sun off that lily-white face of yours."

"Uh, thanks," Carson said, taking the hat, then setting it atop his head. It had been a while since he'd donned a cowboy hat. He had his brother's in his apartment back in San Antonio.

"Now you look like you belong in Prosper," Grandad said.

"About that," Carson said. "You know this visit is not a commitment yet, right?"

Grandad waved a calloused hand. "Finish your chili, then we've got to get moving. Why don't you drive?"

"Sure thing," Carson said. And that's how it was between him and Grandad.

The rodeo arena was larger than Carson expected, and as he walked around it, Grandad talked about upgrading the concessions, adding an extra parking lot on the south side, and other things, but Carson's attention had been distracted by the framed photos in the manager's office.

A couple of the pictures were of a bull rider named Knox Prosper.

Carson studied the action shots. This was Evie's older brother.

"You've heard of Knox Prosper?" Grandad asked, coming to stand by him.

"Not until I met Evie," Carson said. "I guess I'm not up to date on the rodeo circuit."

"Knox Prosper is a legend in this town, or at least he was until he had a falling out with his father."

"The mayor? Really?"

Grandad nodded. "Word is that he took his inheritance on an early draw. Went through a divorce, and his ex-wife married Holt, Knox's older brother."

"Wow," Carson said. "That's a lot of family drama." He'd heard nothing about it from Evie, but why would she tell him in the first place?

"Just prepping you if we decide to go eat at their place tonight."

Carson eyed his grandad. "What do you think?"

"I'm always up for some entertainment."

Carson laughed. "Yes, you are."

After they left the arena, they stopped at the feed store, and Carson loaded up on more gardening implements and fertilizer. "What do you want to plant?"

Grandad rattled off a few things, and Carson bought starters for several vegetables.

The moment they returned to the dilapidated ranch, Carson set up the television, then he told Grandad he'd be working on the garden. "You can take a nap if you want."

"Nap?" Grandad said, as he settled into the overstuffed chair in front of the TV to make sure he could see the screen okay. "When in the Sam have I ever taken a nap?"

Carson chuckled as he rubbed the back of his neck. "It's just a suggestion, Pops."

Grandad waved him off with a grunt, and Carson headed out the back. As he worked, he thought about Evie and what she'd said about Prosper. Yeah, it was a tiny town, but Carson didn't mind that. He was past the years of intense football workouts and playing games. Past the years of high school dating. Past a lot of stuff. Life had changed when he'd lost his brother. Family had always been important, and now it was everything.

He understood Evie's sentiments of wanting to live in a bigger city, but he also wondered where she'd end up. These weren't things he should be dwelling on. Evie was a beautiful woman, an interesting person, and she'd made it clear her mind was made up. Not that it would affect Carson either way. He had no intention of getting involved with a woman at this point in his life. Maybe a couple of years down the road, when more time had passed, and his emotions had settled. And seeing an accident didn't shut him down.

Three hours later, he was in need of a shower, but he'd made a lot of progress in the garden. He'd cleared out all of the dead stuff and turned over the soil, mixing in some fertilizer.

He headed into the house for a drink and found Grandad sound asleep in his chair. Carson left him to his nap and jumped in the shower, then changed. It was nearly six, and when he came out of the bedroom, he hesitated, debating whether or not to wake up his grandad.

But Carson did want to see Evie again, and it was probably a good idea to be a decent neighbor.

"Grandad," Carson said, nudging his shoulder.

The old man's eyes flew open. "Huh? What's happening?"

Carson held back a laugh. "You were asleep."

"Like Sam I was." Grandad pushed off the chair. "What time is it?"

"Ten to six."

"We got a dinner appointment," Grandad said. "What are you waiting for? Come on." He snatched the hat from where he'd left it on the kitchen counter, then strode to the front door. "You're driving again."

Carson shook his head as he followed Grandad. It was always an adventure with him. And he hoped to get some serious time this week to go over the entirety of Grandad's company and make sure this was something he could do and not screw up.

As they drove the short distance to Prosperity Ranch, Grandad continued to talk about Evie's family. All about a little girl named Ruby and how the mayor's other daughter was in some sort of famous culinary school.

When they pulled up close to the driveway, it seemed they'd been heard arriving, and one of Evie's brothers walked out.

He headed straight for the truck as Carson climbed out.

"Carson, right?" he said.

"Right, and you are . . ."

"Lane." His blue eyes were a shade murkier than his sister's. "Holt's in the barn. Wanna come with me for a second?"

Carson glanced over at Grandad, wondering if he was invited, too, or what this invitation was all about.

"Go ahead," Grandad said, "I'll go inside and make myself at home with your mother's lemonade."

Lane grinned. "Sure thing." He clapped a hand on Carson's shoulder, a bit hard. "Let's go."

They walked to the barn, and Carson couldn't help

asking about the ranch. "You've got a real stellar place here. Puts Grandad's place to shame."

"It all takes time," Lane said. "The Andersons have been gone almost ten years, so I'm sure there's a lot of work to do, and we can help."

This Carson hadn't expected. "That would be amazing," he said. "I'm here this week, but then I'm back in school."

"Evie said you're getting a master's?"

"That's right." Carson wondered what else Evie had said about him, and why he liked the notion of her talking about him.

"That's a step in your favor," Lane said.

"What does that mean?"

But they'd reached the entrance of the barn, and Lane called out, "Holt, he's here!"

9

EVIE HAD HEARD THE truck pull into the driveway, but when Mr. Hunt was the only one to come inside, her senses immediately went on alert. Well, more so than they already had at the thought of Carson Hunt eating dinner with practically her entire family. Maybe he hadn't come?

So, she continued slicing the cucumbers for the giant salad she was making, listening to her parents chat with Mr. Hunt.

And then Evie glanced out the kitchen window. There, at the edge of the barn, stood three men. She definitely recognized her two brothers, and it appeared they'd cornered Carson Hunt.

"Oh, no you don't," Evie hissed under her breath. She set down the knife and abandoned the cutting board, then strode out of the kitchen.

Without a word of explanation to anyone, Evie hurried outside, wiping her hands on her apron. *Oh, apron.* She yanked it off and balled it up in one hand. As she neared the men, Holt glanced over at her. Amusement flashed across his face, and that only made Evie angrier.

It was a known thing in Prosper that any guy who wanted

to date a Prosper sister had to answer to the brothers. So help her if her brothers were grilling Carson Hunt. They were absolutely *not* dating, and Evie was no longer a teenager.

"Well, hello, Evie darlin'," Holt said.

"Don't darlin' me, Holt," she said.

He chuckled, totally unfazed that she was about to combust. At the sound of their conversation, the other two men turned.

Lane's smirk was in full force, and Carson simply gazed at her, those nice eyebrows of his raised just a bit.

"To what do we owe this pleasure, sis?" Lane asked. "Is supper on?"

Evie settled her hands on her hips. "Leave Carson alone," she said. "He gave me a ride, that's it. Nothing more. You don't need to ask him about his family, his education, his pedigree, his standards, his former girlfriends, whether he's been convicted of a crime—"

"Whoa, Evie," Holt cut in, placing a hand on her shoulder. "We weren't grilling your friend here about any of that. What do you take us for?"

Evie's breath stopped in her throat as she looked at her brothers. Both of them were holding back laughs. And Carson? He was gazing like she was in a museum exhibit—like he wasn't sure he was believing what he was seeing.

"You're . . . you're not?"

Lane grinned, and Holt chuckled.

Then Evie blushed. All the way to her toes.

"Carson here is helping his grandad," Holt continued, "and we were giving him some advice since the cleanup of their place is much too big for a couple of men to handle."

"Oh." Evie's voice sounded very, very small.

"Why do you always think we're talking about you?" Lane said with a snicker.

Holt's chuckle borderlined a laugh.

Evie pointed at him. "Don't you dare." Then she turned, her apron still balled in her hand, and strode back to the house. Never mind that all three men were certainly watching her every departing step, and would likely burst into laughter as soon as she entered the house.

Whatever. She didn't care. And she couldn't explain to Carson anyway, because it wasn't like she'd be seeing him after dinner was over. He'd brought up her giving him a tour of the town, but that was off the table now.

She might have to spend the week with her family—and she'd somehow survive her two brothers' teasing—but she had no obligation toward Carson. In fact, she'd be taking the bus back to school. Or maybe tell Holt he had to drive her. He certainly owed her that.

Before she reached the porch, a car pulled into the driveway, and out stepped Macie, Holt's wife. Her dark hair waved about her shoulders, and as usual, she looked as pretty as a peach with her brown eyes and honey complexion.

"Hi, Evie," Macie said, hurrying toward her and giving her a hug. Drawing back, she continued, "How are you?" Two lines formed between her brows. "Are you okay?"

So, maybe Evie's eyes were watery with angry tears. Or embarrassed ones. "My brothers are jerks, but what else is new?"

Macie's laughter tinkled, and she slipped an arm about Evie's waist. "Come on. Let's get this dinner over with. We need to hang out together while you're here—just us. We need to catch up on everything."

Evie released a breath, surprisingly feeling better already. Macie was like that. Made people feel comfortable. Evie would focus on spending time with Macie later, and not her annoying brothers and the fact that Carson had been witness to her losing her composure.

She and Macie went into the house, and Ruby catapulted herself at her mom. After a flurry of hugs and kisses, Ruby settled on her grandpa's lap as he continued talking to Mr. Hunt about the arena, and plans for a renovation.

Evie only listened with half an ear as she finished the salad preparations. Her mom and Macie set the table, then Macie pulled out the baked chicken breasts from the oven. Evie began filling glasses with ice water, if only to distract herself from the fact that Carson had just entered the house with her brothers.

The murmur of male voices floated in from the front room, and Evie found herself going hot all over again. Because she still felt embarrassed, and not for any other reason. Not because when she was confronting her brothers, she'd noticed how good Carson looked in a cowboy hat. And not because she'd appreciated his clean shower scent, and the way his long-sleeved shirt was rolled up to his elbows, showing that although he was a grad student, he obviously spent plenty of time outdoors as well. His sculpted forearms also spoke of an athletic past that wasn't so far back in his history.

Now, his voice rose above the others in the front room as he answered a question, apparently about how he'd spent the day. Gardening?

Interesting.

"Looks like everything's ready," her mom said, clapping her hands together. "Evie, will you call the men to the table?"

"Sure," Evie said, although she was reluctant. Pasting a smile on her face, she entered the front room. Her gaze zeroed on her dad and little Ruby. "Dinner's ready, everyone."

Then she turned without making eye contact with anyone else. Moments later, everyone was seated at the table, and Evie had purposely sat next to Ruby, who was perched on her booster chair. She'd be the perfect distraction.

After her father said grace, Evie used the salad tongs to set a portion on Ruby's plate, then hers.

"I don't like salad," Ruby proclaimed.

"Not even cucumbers?" Evie said as she reached for the dressing to drizzle over her own salad. She knew that the dressing would be homemade and delicious. Her mom was the type of cook that made almost everything from scratch. She oversaw all food preparations, keeping the men out of the kitchen until it was time to clean up. Then the dishes were all theirs.

"They're green," Ruby said, as if that was the biggest fault ever.

"They sure are," Evie said, hiding a smile. The other adults were talking about adult stuff, and Evie was perfectly content to chat with a four-year-old. "Do you know what else is green?"

Ruby's eyes rounded. "What?"

"Grapes."

"I like grapes."

Evie smiled. "Me, too. And guess what? Apples are green."

"Sometimes."

"Yep, sometimes. And pears are green."

Ruby looked down at her salad, biting her lip.

"How about you dip the cucumber into the dressing? Then see if you like it." Evie poured a small circle of dressing on the side of Ruby's plate.

Ruby picked up her fork, stabbed a cucumber slice, then dipped it into the dressing. She took a tiny bit and chewed.

"Do you like it?" Evie pressed.

Ruby looked like she didn't quite know, then she smiled. "I love it."

"Yay," Evie said.

"You're a miracle worker," said Macie, who sat on the other side of Ruby. "I don't think she's ever eaten salad without threats before."

Evie smiled as Ruby took another bite, then another.

"It's the dressing," Evie said. "I don't like salad without Mom's dressing either."

She glanced up then and found Carson's gaze on her. His eyes were warm, amused, and Evie tamped down the flash of heat threatening to build. He'd taken off his hat, and his hair was mussed. Adorably.

Evie dug into her own salad. If there was one thing she missed about Prosper, it was her mom's home cooking. Her sister, Cara, had been the one in the family to inherit the talent, although she'd taken it to the extreme. Evie could fix the basics, but hadn't ever really been in charge of a whole dinner. There just wasn't a need for it in college dorm living.

"Can you play dolls with me after dinner?" Ruby asked.

"We have to get home tonight," Macie cut in. "But maybe Evie can spend time with you tomorrow?"

"Tomorrow works for me," Evie said, smiling at Ruby so she wouldn't get her feelings hurt.

Ruby turned to her mom with a smile. "Can Evie sleep over? We can share my princess bed."

"I don't think so, sweetie," Macie said. "I think she'll want her own bed tonight."

The mother and daughter pair continued to talk about why Evie wouldn't be sleeping over, and she truthfully was waiting for the dinner hour to be over. So that Carson and his grandad would leave, and she could have some peace of mind.

Spending all morning with Carson, and now seeing him interact with her family, had taught her that he was the kind of guy who fit in perfectly in a small town like Prosper. He was personable, helpful to his grandad, interested in what others had to say, full of knowledge of his own, and well . . . insanely good-looking. Which probably meant that with one night on the town—i.e. an appearance at Racoons—all the single women would flock to him.

And Evie wouldn't blame them. Carson Hunt was a catch, the real deal, and there must be some wealth in his family if his grandad was buying up arenas left and right.

"Tell us about how you met," Evie's mother said.

Wow. This had already been gone over. More than once. But now her mom was looking from Carson to Evie as if she expected some juicy story of meeting each other and falling in love at first sight.

Carson's gaze was on her again, those brown eyes amused, and thinking who knew what.

"At school, Mom," Evie said, passing along the bowl of fresh rolls. "I told you that."

"I know, dear," her mom said. "But how? Are you in a class together?"

Evie refrained from rolling her eyes. "Mom, I'm in the final classes of my graphics art major, and Carson is a graduate student. What do you think?"

"Evelyn," her father said.

Great. Now her dad was chastising her in front of company. Was it just her, or was she being treated like a little kid in her own home?

"If you answer the question, then Mom will stop asking so many," Lane said, his voice about a half-step away from laughter.

Evie glared at Lane. Who cared if Carson Hunt witnessed a little sibling strife? It wasn't like she was trying to impress him or anything. Besides, her brother of all people knew her mom would never stop with the questions.

"Why don't you tell us, Carson?" Holt cut in.

All eyes shifted to him. And that's when Evie started praying that Carson Hunt wouldn't tell the exact details of their first meeting. Because it had been mortifying enough. And her parents would probably be shocked to know that she'd been at such a wild party. No, her parents weren't naïve, but college partying wasn't something they needed to discuss at the dinner table.

"Sure thing," Carson started to say.

Evie focused her full attention on him, wishing that he could read her mind. *Don't say anything. Make up something. I don't care what.*

But Carson did say something.

"We met through her roommate, Becca," he said.

Evie's breath nearly left her chest. He wasn't going to bring up Devon and the football party?

"Becca and I study at the library every morning," Carson said. "Not together, but in the same area. And the other day, Evie showed up with her." He shrugged as he picked up his water glass. "It became a really small world when I found out Evie was from Prosper."

His grandad slapped him on the back. "Small world, indeed, boy."

"How about that? A really small world," Lane said, an edge of suspicion in his tone. Didn't he believe Carson?

"Right," Evie said, and all eyes shifted to her now. "The library. I don't usually go in the mornings because I'm a night owl, I guess."

"How nice that you decided to go with Becca, then," her mom said.

Evie had no idea why Carson had covered for her, but she owed him, big time. He and Holt started talking about the horses Holt was training, but Evie knew that Carson was aware of her. Did he understand how much of a bullet he'd helped her dodge?

The last thing she wanted to do was explain who Devon was and how she'd gotten into a situation that could have been much, much worse if it wasn't for Carson Hunt forcing that door open.

The rest of the meal was a blur as Evie's thoughts raced. She was more curious now than grateful. Why had he said what he'd said? When dinner ended, she was still feeling antsy. Not so much for Carson to leave, but for her family to mind their own business, so that she could go over to his grandad's property and talk to Carson alone.

But the evening continued surrounded by people, even though Holt, Macie, and Ruby had gone back to Holt's house in town, and Carson and Mr. Hunt left. She listened to her mom talk about a new quilt she was starting up while Lane and her dad did the dishes. Then her dad went off to some meeting, and that left Lane and her mom choosing a historical western movie to watch.

Evie didn't feel like she could bow out without another round of questions, so she settled on the couch and half-watched a jilted son try to get revenge on his father.

10

THE NIGHT SKY SEEMED to swallow the earth, and the stars were impossible to count. It was something that Carson had forgotten about over the last few years of school and football and figuring out how to see a future that didn't include Rhett.

"You lock up when you come to bed," Grandad hollered through the screen door. "I'm heading off to bed. I'm not as young as I used to be."

"Okay, Pops, will do." Although, Carson was sure locking up wasn't entirely necessary. There was nothing at this old homestead to steal, and Prosper didn't strike him as a place where burglars abounded. But he was used to his grandad's odd ways, and it was always better to agree with him. For the most part.

Carson returned his attention to the vast sky from where he sat sprawled on a wooden deck chair on the back patio. He should get to bed soon, too. It had been a long day, and if his grandad still had his old habits, they'd both be up by dawn, working on one thing or another.

The glittering stars above brought a peace that was hard to explain. It was more than welcome, especially after witnessing that motorcycle crash earlier that day. Evie had helped him out more than she could know, and he didn't know if he could explain it to her, ever, but just driving the rest of the way and not asking questions had been exactly what he needed.

Now, looking back and having some emotional distance, Carson realized that he'd been triggered. PTSD, or something? He wasn't sure. He wasn't the expert. But the accident had hit close to home, and all he'd been able to think about was if someone had been there to help his brother sooner, then maybe Rhett would still be alive.

The sound of car tires on gravel caught Carson's attention. Someone was pulling up to the house. It was late, especially for a sleepy little town, and he didn't want his grandad bothered unless it was necessary. A lifetime of living with the old man had taught Carson not to wake his grandad—the man became something fierce when startled from sleep.

So Carson rose and walked around the house. He reached the front corner of the house just as someone climbed out of a car. The silhouette against the moonlight told him it was a woman.

"Evie?" he said in a soft voice.

She jumped. "Carson. You scared me!"

He walked toward her, hands in his jeans pockets. "You're the one who's here in the dead of night. You scared me."

She watched him approach, and in the moonlight, he couldn't read her eyes, but her mouth had curved upward.

"Sorry about scaring you," she said, her tone teasing. "I didn't realize how late it was. Were you . . . asleep?"

Obviously not, but he'd play along. "Not yet. I'm stargazing. Wanna join me?"

He felt her surprise rather than saw it.

"Right now?"

"Well, the stars are out," he said. "So there's no time like the present. Plus, it seems that neither of us are sleeping, so . . ." He held out his hand—why, he didn't know. Because it was dark, maybe, and she wasn't familiar with the landscape?

She hesitated, as he suspected she would, then she placed her hand in his. Her fingers were cool and smooth. And he wrapped his larger hand around hers and pulled her with him.

"Come on," he said. "The best place is on the back patio. There're a couple of chairs there, too."

"Okay."

He led her around the side of the house, and she didn't pull away from his grasp. What was she thinking? What was *he* thinking? He liked this. Spontaneous as it was. He liked it very much.

When they reached the patio, he motioned toward one of the chairs, and she released his hand and sat down. By the time he settled into the nearby chair, she'd tilted her chin up and was staring at the sky. So he did, too.

He could make out a few of the constellations, the major ones, but he'd never paid much attention to astronomy. Maybe that would change if he decided to live in Prosper. Neither of them were speaking, and he wondered how long he'd have to wait before Evie told him why she'd come over. It wasn't like he should be flattered or anything—okay, so maybe he was a little. Or a lot.

She'd come to see him, right? Talk to him? Ask him for a favor? Discuss what had happened at her family's ranch? Tell him why she'd come unglued on her brothers in front of him, *over* him? Carson hadn't minded in the least. Warmth buzzed through him at the thought.

It took maybe four minutes, or five, before she started talking. "Why did you tell my family that we met in the library?"

Ah, that.

"Well, I weighed my options, and you seemed to already be bothered by your mom asking you the question, so I decided I'd take the neutral approach." He paused. "Should I have told them about the football party?"

"No," she said quickly. "I don't need to feel like an idiot more than I already do."

"You're not an idiot," Carson said.

Evie scoffed. "I followed after Devon like a lost dog, and when he asked me out, I thought I'd be different. You know, different from the party girls he always dates. I thought he'd see *me*. Be interested. Intrigued. And not treat me like all the other flighty women after him."

Carson blew out a breath. "Guys like that don't grow up for a long time. Some of them never do. They end up hurting others and leaving hurricane-like destruction in their paths."

"Yeah, I understand that now," Evie said. "Loud and clear. I mean, I almost had my first kiss from a guy who probably doesn't even know my last name."

She covered her mouth and mumbled, "I didn't mean to say that."

Carson glanced over at her. Had she just said . . . was it possible? "What part didn't you mean to say? The not knowing the last name part or . . ."

Evie bolted from the chair and took off around the house.

"Evie," Carson said. "Where are you going?" He followed, jogging around the house to barely catch up with her as she reached for the handle of her car door.

She opened the door, but before she could slip inside and drive away, Carson grasped her arm. "Evie?"

She turned to face him, and he dropped his hand. Her eyes were wide, as if she were spooked about something.

She folded her arms. "I don't know why I told you that.

Becca barely found out the other day. If you say anything, to anyone, so help me . . ."

Her voice was trembling, and Carson didn't know what to make of it. "I won't say anything. Besides, who would I tell?"

"All you have to do is tell one person in Prosper, and everyone will know it," Evie said, her voice cracking.

Carson raised both his hands. "I swear, I won't say a thing."

Evie stared at him, and he gazed right back.

"Promise?"

"Promise."

She exhaled and unfolded her arms. Then she wiped at her cheeks.

Was she crying now? Carson had no idea what to do.

"You probably think I'm overreacting," she said in a quiet voice, wiping at her cheeks again, "and you probably think I'm a bratty sister to my brothers. But they . . . they're part of the reason that I never dated before college, except for one lousy prom that went completely wrong. And it's probably why I'm making poor choices about guys now."

Carson wanted to dry her tears, maybe pull her into a hug, but he could feel the tension radiating from her. And he didn't want her to think he was coming onto her, even though she looked beautiful in the moonlight. "I don't think you're a bratty sister, Evie. You should have seen how my brother and I fought. I mean, we were always bickering about something."

She seemed too distressed and caught up in her own emotional turmoil to catch onto his past tense referral of his brother. Her gaze had slipped away, and she was biting her lip.

"Look," Carson said. "I don't want to stir up things between you and your brothers. If you don't want me over at the ranch tomorrow, then I've got plenty to do with my grandad."

Her gaze lifted, and her brows arched. "They invited you over?"

"Yeah."

She bit that pretty lip of hers again, and Carson wondered how in the world, whether in high school or in all her years at college, this woman had never been kissed. But right now, he knew it wasn't a question he could pursue. She was still upset.

"Hey," he hedged. "Your brothers are good guys from what I know, and they're just protective, even though it comes across as strong. I mean, they wouldn't drill a guy you're going out with unless they cared."

She wrinkled her nose. "I know. They care too much, though."

Carson tried not to smile, but failed.

"You're laughing at me," Evie said, her eyes narrowing.

"I'm not laughing at you," he said. "You're just adorable when you scrunch up your face like that."

Now, she glowered. "You did not just say that."

Carson was grinning now. Glowering was better than crying. "I did just say that. But really, you're a beautiful woman, Evie, so no wonder your brothers are protective. There's a lot of jerks out there."

"You're just trying to make me feel better."

Had Carson ever met a more stubborn person? "I do want you to feel better, sweetness, but that doesn't mean I'm not telling the truth."

She studied him. "I already know the truth. I'm awkward, and apparently naïve, when it comes to dating. I don't know where I'll be living in two months. I cave to pressure and can't seem to stand on my own two feet. I'm pathetic, really."

Carson would have never guessed in a hundred years that all of these thoughts ran through Evie's mind.

"Can I see your phone?" he asked.

Lines appeared between her brows. "Why?"

"So I can text you something, and then you can read it over and over and not forget it."

She hesitated, and he could practically see the arguments flitting across her face. Her beautiful face.

Finally, she pulled out her phone from her back pocket and handed it to him. He opened the contacts and added his name and number, then he texted his own phone, which he'd left in the house. He handed it back.

"Do I get the grand tour of Prosper tomorrow?" he asked. "Or what?"

She slipped her phone into her pocket again. "Maybe."

"Okay . . ."

She shrugged. "I'm helping my mom with her quilt, and Macie wants to hang out at some point, but I might have ten minutes to show you the rest of Prosper."

He chuckled, and he loved when she smiled. How Evie didn't know how beautiful she was, when she smiled, laughed, cried, or even yelled at her brothers, Carson couldn't figure it out. "Well, let me know when you have ten minutes free. I'll take a break from whatever Grandad has on his list of chores for me."

Evie looked at the house, and Carson saw what she saw: a rundown homestead in need of a major facelift.

"I'm sure your grandad is grateful you're here to help." Then she looked at him. "Thanks, Carson, for, uh, covering for me. I'm glad I don't have to explain to my family about the football party. As you know, they're nosy and overprotective enough."

"Sure thing."

She stepped away then and slid into the driver's seat.

Carson moved back from the car and watched her drive down the road that connected to the street leading to her family's ranch. Then he went inside the house to find his phone. He waited a few minutes before he sent a text to her number so that it would go through when she wasn't still driving.

After another minute, her reply finally came.

You can hang out with my brothers if you want.

He grinned. *What about our ten-minute tour?*

I think I can work you in around noon.

11

EVIE COULD HEAR THE early-morning movements about the house as she stayed burrowed beneath a quilt. Holt had already arrived, and it sounded like he must be having coffee with her dad and Lane. Her mom wasn't up yet, and it surprised Evie. And worried her, too. Was it because of the cancer? Her mom was in remission now, but there was always the fear that it would come back.

Evie slipped one hand out of the covers and snatched her cell phone, then brought it into her cocoon of blankets. She looked at the recent activity on her phone. Nothing more from Becca. They'd texted a couple of times last night—before Evie had gone over to Carson's. Instagram was filled with vacation pictures from everyone she followed at college.

Apparently, no one had gone back home to their family ranch.

Evie checked her email and found that a couple of her assignments had been graded. She opened up the links. B+ and A-. Good enough. She wasn't a straight-A student like Becca, and never would be, but graphic art could be subjective, anyway.

Evie should shut off her phone now, maybe go back to

sleep for an hour. It was barely after 6:00 a.m., and if her mom wasn't awake yet and didn't need help with something, then it was a reprieve for Evie. After all, it was spring break.

Instead, she didn't shut off her phone, but pulled up the text from Carson. The one he'd sent last night, and the one she'd read at least a dozen times, or two dozen, before finally falling asleep.

You want the truth? Here's the truth. The most beautiful women are the ones who don't realize it. You're not only beautiful on the outside, but you're beautiful on the inside. If you didn't have a good heart, you wouldn't feel so torn about choosing where to work after graduation. Even though you say you don't want to live in Prosper, I can see how much your family means to you. You aren't awkward, not in the least. You're finding your footing. Big decisions are looming, and you're testing the waters. If you're naïve, it's because you see only the good in people and trust too much. And if you think you cave to pressure, you don't. You're choosing what you think is the best thing for everyone. I should be thanking you, Evie Prosper, because it's been a long time since I've enjoyed the company of a woman who didn't have an agenda. Maybe it's even the first time. I'm not lying when I say you're beautiful, and you should know that you're stronger than you think.

Okay, so she was teary again—had been last night, too, when reading it over and over.

Carson should be a professional letter writer or greeting card creator—was there such a profession? On one hand, the text was completely cheesy; on the other hand, it had reached her deepest insecurities. His words were perhaps the most sincere she'd ever heard from a guy—from anyone, really.

She closed her eyes for a moment, ignoring the sounds about the house as she absorbed all that was Carson. His smile that she was seeing more and more of. The way he was so direct in his words. His surprising vulnerability. That motorcycle accident had been rough on him, and she was glad she could help him by driving.

She liked how he seemed at ease with all types of people. He hadn't been fazed by anything in her family—not her brothers' intrusive questions or their apparent instant friendship. She'd made it clear to her brothers that Carson was just a random ride, nothing more. But now . . . *Stop, Evie!* She had a problem, and she knew it. A guy paid a little attention to her, and suddenly, she was dreaming up a happily ever after. She had to stop doing that. Especially with Carson. He knew her family. His grandad was their next-door neighbor, and Carson could very well be a Prosper resident soon.

She also knew his text by heart, and how he'd implied that other women—Ones he'd dated? Had relationships with?—always had an agenda. And he appreciated that she didn't. So she wasn't going to think about how holding his hand last night for those brief moments had sent goose bumps skittering across her skin. Or how the deep timbre of his voice had made her feel all melty inside. And how when he said she was beautiful, she could have thrown her arms about his neck and never let go.

Her phone buzzed, and Evie opened the incoming text from Becca.

What's the update?

Evie groaned. She might have said too much about Carson yesterday, and she might have told Becca she was going over to his homestead to talk to him last night. She typed out a short reply, because she wasn't ready to explain to Becca. She'd just analyze every little thing, and Evie had done enough of that on her own.

Nothing new. Just woke up. Helping my mom today with her new quilt.

Will you see Carson?

Probably, but don't read into it.

I'm totally reading into it.

Evie sighed. *I know you are. But I'm not going to be.*

Becca sent a winking emoji.

And before Evie could be tempted to re-read Carson's text to her, she climbed out of bed. The house had gone silent, which meant the men were outside someplace. After her shower, Evie went into the kitchen to find cold coffee. She put on new coffee and found some eggs in the fridge. She made extra scrambled eggs for her mom, then covered the bowl so she would find it when she woke up.

"Evie?" her mom said.

She turned to see her mom in her robe and slippers, not a sight she often saw. She was always put together. "Sleep in?" Evie teased, although she felt a knot of worry tightening her stomach.

Her mom smiled. "No, I like to read in bed for about an hour. Besides, 7:00 am is early in most people's lives."

"Right." Evie began to wash out her bowl and the pan and utensils she'd used. "When do you want to start on the quilt?"

Her mom sat at the kitchen table. "After your ride."

"My ride?" Evie looked over her shoulder. "What are you talking about?"

"Go on and ride your horse," her mom said. "Enjoy yourself while you're here."

"But I thought—"

"The quilt is just something fun we can do together," her mom said. "I'm not on a deadline or anything. Besides, I'm going to start on preparations for lunch, then dinner." She dug into the bowl of scrambled eggs and took a bite. "Thanks for this, it's delicious."

"Mom, I can help you with whatever you want," Evie

said, setting her hands on her hips. "I know I'm on spring break, but I don't want you taking care of everyone when we can do that for ourselves."

Her mom gazed at her with a soft smile. "I like doing things for my family. And you know, cooking is my thing, my therapy."

And Evie knew that, but didn't her mom need a break? "Why don't you ride with me?"

"I haven't ridden for a while," her mom said. "I have my full strength back, but I don't trust myself on a horse. But really, you go. Enjoy the fresh air of the country."

Evie crossed to her mom and bent to kiss her temple. "Okay, see you soon. And I have my phone with me."

When Evie stepped out into the morning, decked in the cowboy boots she'd pulled out of her closet, her oldest jeans, and a well-worn flannel shirt, the familiar scents of the ranch struck. The new grass, the spring flowers, the fresh air, and even the tang of the horse arena. It all brought on a wave of nostalgia, feeling like home.

Evie strode to the barn and walked inside to find Jerry, their ranch hand, brushing down the horses.

"Hi, Miss Evie," he said, turning a wide grin toward her. He was a short, wiry man, with dark hair and eyes.

"Hi, Jerry," she said. "Where is everyone?"

"They all went into town to the feed store," he said. "Lane was talking big about bringing in some new type of vitamin mix that will be good for the horses."

Ah, Lane always had ideas for the ranch, although he claimed never to want to work here.

"How are the horses?" Evie asked as she walked toward the stable.

"They're great," Jerry said. "We've got four we're boarding, and Holt is doing their training."

Holt had earned a decent reputation for training horses for different rodeo events. It helped that they had their own small arena at the ranch, and then of course, access to the main rodeo arena in town.

She spotted her favorite gray mare, Molly. "Hey, girl."

Molly nudged Evie's shoulder as she stroked her long nose. Evie laughed. "Does that mean you missed me?"

"Wanna take her for a ride?" Jerry asked.

"Sure," Evie said. "We both need the exercise."

Jerry brought over the tack, and soon, Evie had Molly saddled. Then she grasped the reins and led the horse out of the stable and through the back of the barn. After she climbed onto Molly, they set off at a walk around the arena.

Holt had created his own little dynasty over the past couple of years. Evie was impressed. The entire ranch seemed to be well-run, and her family content. Having only Lane around on a holiday was a big change. Usually on breaks, Cara was here, too, and Evie always felt insecure around her sister. And Knox . . . Well, he was a different story. He'd cut himself off from the family for so long that Evie was used to him being gone. Since Holt and Macie's wedding, Knox had reached out more to the family at large, which basically meant he participated in group texts.

Since Knox was Ruby's real father, Evie had thought he might come around more just because his daughter lived in Prosper now. But so far, that hadn't happened. He'd basically relegated their relationship to phone calls, which was sort of understandable since he was on the rodeo circuit in Montana.

"Wanna go faster?" Evie asked the horse.

Molly tossed her head.

"I'll take that as a *yes*," Evie said with a laugh, and snapped the reins. "Come on."

Molly moved to a canter, and Evie gazed about the

landscape. On the west side of the property was a river, and she headed toward it. Before reaching the copse of trees, she reangled Molly and continued south. Now, she was technically on the old Anderson property—well, now Mr. Hunt's, and she supposed Carson's.

She slowed the horse to a walk as she checked out her surroundings. The spring grass stretched as far as she could see, and butterflies and insects moved lazily about the wildflowers. The morning sun had finally dried the dew, and the endless blue sky promised plenty of warmth later.

Without realizing it, Evie had traveled quite a bit farther onto the Hunts' property. In fact, she could see the back of the house, and . . .

Carson was standing in the backyard, in the garden? His back was to her, and well, she knew it was him, because surely his grandad didn't have such broad, muscled shoulders, and a back that was magazine-worthy. Because, yep, Carson was shirtless. He stood, hands on his hips, as he surveyed whatever he was looking at.

Evie was staring—how could she not? She might be caught at any moment, but her hands were frozen on the reins. Even the horse seemed mesmerized by the shirtless Carson Hunt.

"We need to leave," Evie whispered to her horse.

Molly didn't reply.

Carson lifted a hand and scrubbed his fingers through his hair, then he leaned down and tossed something forward. Beyond him, yellow flames leapt up.

Oh, he was burning garden mulch.

He took a couple of steps away and folded his arms as he watched the burning heap.

He was engrossed, and Evie could turn around and leave without being noticed. She was about to do just that when the back door to the house opened, and Mr. Hunt stepped out.

"Breakfast is ready," he hollered. "What in the Sam are you doing, son?"

"Burning some dead plants. I'll be there when this is out," Carson told his grandad.

"Hello, Evie," Mr. Hunt said, his gaze finding her across the property. Then he ducked into the house, the door shutting after him.

Oh, no. It was absolutely too late to sneak away.

Sure enough, Carson turned around, shielding his eyes against the rising sun.

Evie jerked the reins, and Molly took a couple of steps backward. Evie really wanted to turn and gallop away, but that would look like she was in the wrong or something, and although she was technically trespassing, it wasn't like she wasn't welcome, right?

"Hey," Carson said.

"Hey."

His smile started slow, then grew. Evie was definitely blushing. That smile, combined with what he was wearing—or *not* wearing to be more exact—definitely had her heating up all over. She was doing it again. Forming a crush on an unattainable guy. If there was anyone who was unattainable, it was Carson Hunt. He was a small-town guy who'd be settling in Prosper of all places.

And . . . Carson was walking toward her. The sun gleamed off his hair and shoulders and torso and abs and forearms and biceps and . . .

"Are you okay?" he asked.

"Yeah." Although, she was basically frozen in place.

Carson stopped near the horse. "Hi, pretty lady."

It took her a second to realize he was talking to the horse.

"What's her name?" he asked.

"Molly."

Carson looked up at her, and this close, she could see the lighter brown in his eyes. "Want to come in for breakfast? Grandad's been hard at work on the stove this morning."

"Uh, I already ate," she said. Did she sound breathless? "Thanks, though. I should get going. My mom needs help, and I didn't mean to ride out this far."

Carson didn't look like he believed her for one minute, but he stepped away from the horse.

Evie dragged her gaze away from the perfection that was his body and urged Molly to turn around. The horse obeyed, and soon, Evie was pushing her into a gallop because she really needed the wind to cool off her face. She thought she heard Carson chuckle, but she didn't look back to find out.

When Evie neared the barn of her family ranch, she climbed off Molly and led her to the water trough. "What do you think about Carson?" she asked her horse.

The horse continued to drink, oblivious to Evie's spinning thoughts. Carson had to know he had an effect on her. It wasn't like he'd known she was coming over—thus, he was shirtless—but when he saw her, he could have just waved instead of walking to meet her. And that smile of his . . . Evie sighed.

"Everything okay?" Lane's voice cut into her unbidden thoughts.

She turned with a start to see her brother heading out of the barn. "Oh, you're back. That's great."

Lane's brows pulled together. "You're acting weird, sis."

"I am not," she said immediately, although her cheeks were starting to burn hot. Could her brother read her mind? *Was* she acting weird?

Lane folded his arms. "Just admit it, you like him."

"*Him?*"

"You know who I mean."

And she did. Evie kept her shoulders stiff, her expression neutral, her eyes on the horse. "So what are your plans the rest of the day?"

Lane scoffed, since he likely knew she was trying to change the subject. "Carson's coming over, and I want to run a business deal past him."

"Of course you do." The words were matter-of-fact, without malice. Just because Lane was still in college himself didn't mean he wasn't full of ideas on improving the profitability of the ranch.

"You can hang out with us if you want," Lane said, nudging her shoulder.

She could hear the smile in his voice without even looking at him.

"We'll see," she said simply. *Over her dead body.*

12

IT WAS NOON, AND Carson probably shouldn't be obsessing over the time, but he was. Currently, he was leaning against the arena wall at Prosperity Ranch as Lane talked about the improvements Holt had made over the past year. It was all interesting, and definitely smart. The two brothers had created the beginnings of an empire. Holt used to do a lot of traveling to train skittish horses, but now the horses were coming to him. Some for weeks. Others for a few days.

Lane had somehow secured a grant that paid for the room and board of neglected horses, and they were now thinking about expanding. He had one more semester before he graduated in finance, and he was already putting his education to good use. It was pretty cool to see how Holt respected his younger brother's opinions. Their relationship reminded him of his own brother.

"So do you think your grandad might be interested in setting up a couple of stables to help with the boarding?" Lane asked. "We'd rent out the stables from him, of course, and do all the work. I just know my mom wouldn't want every inch of our property covered with horses."

"I don't see why not," Carson said. "We could ask him today, if you want."

"Great," Lane said, clapping him on the shoulder. "Why don't you two come over for dinner tonight, and we can discuss it."

Another dinner invite? "Don't you need to clear it with your mom?"

"Oh, don't worry, she'll be more than happy to have the two Hunt men over again." Lane stepped away from the arena wall. "I'm going to find Holt and tell him that you're definitely open to housing our horses."

Carson was very interested in hearing about why Mrs. Prosper would be so happy to have him and Pops over for dinner again, but he didn't think he could ask without raising questions.

Besides, it was after the time that Evie had said she'd take him on a tour of Prosper. Well, she hadn't exactly been definitive, but Carson was counting her text from last night. Seeing her this morning had been . . . well, amazing. He'd been thinking of her that morning, and then suddenly, she burst onto the scene, just like the surge of flames consuming the garden mulch.

And he'd seen the interest in her eyes and the pink stain of her cheeks as he walked toward her. Evie had been wearing slim jeans, boots, and a button-down shirt that made her cuter than any rodeo queen he'd ever seen. She'd braided her hair, and the wisps had danced about her face from the breeze. She looked so natural on a horse, so at ease, that his pulse might have raced a little bit faster.

Evie had no idea how beautiful she was, and Carson needed to look past his attraction to her, or he'd be moving backward in his life. Down the path of heartache and destroyed expectations. There was a reason he hadn't dated since Stacee. He'd had enough of loss and heartbreak in the last couple of years. He'd been trying to put that behind him and not let it rule his life.

And Evie Prosper was a walking land mine. She'd been more than clear about her aversion to living a small-town life. Well . . . it wasn't like Carson was going to propose marriage on the spot. He chuckled to himself. No way. Evie was . . . she was . . . well, innocent and trusting and stubborn, that was for sure. He still couldn't believe she'd never been kissed.

"What's so funny?"

Carson snapped his head around to see Evie herself leaning against the rail, her blue eyes light today.

His mouth went dry. "What are you talking about?"

One of her eyebrows lifted. "I heard you laugh, so I was wondering what you're laughing about."

"Oh, that." His heart was racing. Was that normal? "I can't remember."

Evie scoffed, then turned to look across the arena. "Then what are you looking at?"

"Nothing," Carson said. "I was waiting for you."

She wasn't looking at him, but the edge of her mouth lifted. "You really want a tour that bad? You know, you could have asked one of my brothers, or even my dad."

"I want you to show me your town."

Her brow wrinkled, but there was a warmth in her eyes. "Like I said, it will take ten minutes."

"Are you busy?" he asked.

She turned more fully toward him, and a few wisps of her blonde hair stirred against her jaw. She smelled a lot sweeter than he probably did, even though he'd showered after the garden work that morning.

"I'm always busy," she said, as if she were impatient, but there was a lightness to her tone. "Let's go, if you insist."

"Okay, then I insist."

She spun away from him and headed around the barn, toward the front of the house. Carson caught up with her in a few easy strides.

"We're taking your truck," she announced, veering toward it.

"You know, it's kind of an old truck," he teased.

She rolled her eyes, and he laughed. When her mouth expanded into a smile, he felt his heart expanding at the same time. *Easy, Carson. She doesn't belong to you, or to Prosper.*

Carson reached the truck a step ahead of her, and he opened the passenger door. He wanted to pull her close as she passed by him, if only to breathe in her sweet scent. Or smooth her hair back from her face, or maybe even kiss the edge of that pretty mouth of hers.

Breathe, Carson. And calm down.

He shut the door and walked around the truck, then keeping his gaze forward, he started the truck and drove off the property. As he drove along Main Street, Evie pointed out the various shops, but Carson was barely listening. What was wrong with him? He'd wanted this tour, but he wasn't even paying attention. His mind was full of all things Evie. How she was sitting in his truck, where her hand was resting on the bench not far from him, how the breeze coming through the half-open window tugged at her braid, how she wore light pink nail polish . . .

"And this is the school my mom wants me to work at. Apparently, they have a need for a graphic designer."

Carson shifted his gaze to the brick red school on the other side of the street. The two-story building with its rows of windows was both graceful and stoic. The lawn in front was green and extended to the small parking lot in front. "You went to school here?"

"Yep," Evie said with a sigh. "It's so small that everyone knows everyone else. My graduating class was only thirty-nine kids."

"Wow." Carson looked over at her. The forlorn expression on her face made him curious. He slowed the truck and stopped in full view of the school. "Was it really that bad?"

Evie shifted her gaze to him, and he marveled at how the blue of her eyes could morph into so many shades. "Define bad. When you have three older brothers who are popular and good at everything, and all the girls want to date, yeah, I had no real friends. And every guy who I liked wouldn't dare talk to me, let alone ask me out, because Holt and Knox would give them the riot act. Oh, and it was a total double standard, because I think Knox went through a different girlfriend every week."

"Did you ever talk to your parents about it?"

"Ha," Evie said. "What teenage girl tattles on her brothers to parents who idolize the boys in the family? I mean, my mom still thinks Knox walks on water even after he cheated on his own wife."

Carson blinked. This, he hadn't expected. "Is that why they divorced?"

"Yeah," Evie said. "Of course, there's more to it than that, but it's all in the past now, and my family is trying to move on."

"That sounds rough."

She nodded. "So, my mom's already talked to the principal and everything, and I promised that I'd meet with her tomorrow. Just to make my mom happy, of course."

"Of course." Carson didn't really know what to tell Evie. Well, he knew what he *wanted* to tell her, but he shouldn't. She was already getting enough pressure from her mom, and Carson telling her to consider Prosper would be purely for selfish reasons on his part.

Because Evie moving back to Prosper, and living and working here, sounded like the most perfect thing ever.

"What do *you* want, Evie?" he asked. "I mean, if you could orchestrate the rest of the year, what would it look like?"

She cast a sideways glance at him, and he was surprised to see her cheeks flood with color. "That's the problem. I've applied to several places, as well as my dream job—at the major newspaper office in San Antonio. The places that have gotten back to me are at the bottom of my list as far as what I'm looking for. One's near Dallas, which feels too far away. Ironic, I know. But it would be nice to be only an hour away from home. It's a Catch-22, since everyone wants experience, you know?"

"Maybe you need to settle for something before you get the position you really want."

She nodded. "Maybe."

"Could you get the experience in Prosper?" he asked, testing the waters.

Her gaze narrowed. "Have you been talking to my mom?"

"Nope." He hid a smile. "Think about it. You have established relationships here already, and so they'll likely hire you. Once you have some experience, maybe a year or two, then you'll have a stronger resume to apply for the newspaper in San Antonio, or somewhere else."

"A year or two, huh?"

His smile appeared anyway. "Yep."

She was watching him, and his heart was racing. He reached for her hand, even though he knew it was risking a lot. They were parked in his truck, and he wasn't leading her anywhere, or at least not technically.

"I think it's something worth considering," he said. She hadn't pulled her hand away, so he decided that was a good thing.

"I don't know," she said. "Being home scrambles my brain. My brothers annoy me like crazy, but I love being around my mom. I guess I just appreciate her like I never have before, even if she does ask a lot of questions about you."

This both surprised and pleased Carson. "About *me*?"

"Yeah." Evie glanced down at their linked hands, and yeah, he could pretty much read her mind. *What's happening here?* He was wondering the same thing.

"I need to get back home," she said, "and I'm sure your grandpa needs more mulch burned or something."

He chuckled. Point taken. He released her hand and turned the truck around, wondering if something between him and Evie Prosper was just starting up, or already ending.

13

EVIE REALLY SHOULDN'T BE making a habit of slipping over to the Hunt property at midnight. But the moon had been peeking through the clouds for the past hour, reminding her of the stargazing from last night, and so she'd finally climbed out of bed and left the house. One thing led to another, and before she knew it, she was in her mom's car, driving off the property.

Would Carson be awake? What would he think of her sudden appearance again?

He and his grandpa had come over for dinner again, and the entire conversation had been about Mr. Hunt building some corrals on his land, and Holt boarding more horses there. Everyone seemed to be in favor, and the discussions went long past dinner. Evie had listened, with only partial interest though, since her mind could only focus on how Carson's gaze kept moving to her.

Was it possible for a man to be better looking with every passing hour? Or was she just letting her crush on Carson get out of control? He'd held her hand in the truck, and he'd suggested she give Prosper a try. Was it because he wanted to be around her more? Was she reading too much into it? Why else would he hold her hand?

Evie was terrible at reading signals, she decided.

So, this was the real reason she was pulling up to the Hunt house so late at night. If Carson did come out of the house, then yeah, she was going to ask him point blank. *Do you like me? Why did you hold my hand?*

She took a deep breath and climbed out of the car. It was then she realized that she wasn't exactly wearing normal clothes. Her PJ shorts and oversized sweatshirt were something to lounge in bed with, but not to pay a late-night visit to a very hot male.

And . . . there he was. Sitting on the top step of the porch, as if he'd been . . . waiting for her?

"Hi," she said as he rose to his feet. "Sorry I didn't tell you I was coming over. I needed to ask you a couple of things. Away from my family." She might be talking too fast, but it seemed easier that way.

He hadn't said a word, but just walked toward her, all hunky and tall in the moonlight. At least he had a shirt on, so that was very, very good. He still had his boots on, but no cowboy hat. The earlier breeze of the day had grown into a stronger wind, and his button-down shirt rippled against his torso.

"I'm glad I didn't wake you, though," she said because he still wasn't talking, but she could feel the intensity of his gaze.

He stopped in front of her, his thumbs hooked into the belt loops of his jeans. "What would you have done if you had?"

Evie bit her lip. What kind of question was that? "Apologize?"

The edge of his mouth lifted, and her heart skipped a beat, or two or three.

"I wouldn't have minded," he said.

"If I apologized or woke you up?"

He lifted his shoulders. "Either. Although the clouds are covering the stars tonight, so that sky's not much to look at." He was studying her face, as if he wanted to read her thoughts. "What did you need to ask me?"

"Uh," she started, her earlier gumption fading fast. It was darker than usual tonight with the clouds, and although the moonlight peeked through, they were surrounded by the cool, black night. She was also noticing the scruff on his jaw, and she guessed he hadn't shaved since spring break started. It made him look more rugged, more cowboy-like—the type she'd sworn off because they stayed in small towns. "I guess I wanted to know why you're being so nice to me."

His forehead creased. "What do you mean?"

What *did* she mean? "Well, I can't figure out why you're being so nice to me. Do you like me, or are you just in cahoots with my family and trying to talk me into coming back to Prosper?"

"I barely know your family."

"I know, but they can be very persuasive." She set her hands on her hips. "I mean, my dad is the mayor, and my brothers are going into business with your grandpa, and my mom has fed you dinner twice."

Carson was still staring at her, like he wasn't sure how to answer. Then he smiled.

"What? Are they bribing you or something?"

Carson ran a hand through his hair, then shook his head. "You're something else, Evie Prosper."

"What's that supposed to mean?"

He stepped closer and lowered his head, his voice quiet when he said, "You really came over here to ask me if your family was bribing me to be nice to you so that you'd want to move back to Prosper?"

Evie swallowed. "Yes?" She inched back because Carson had moved closer again. Her back brushed the side of the car. Any closer, and they'd be touching. She caught his scent of musk and soap.

"Evie," he said, his voice a low rumble. Had he always said her name like that? "The answer is no, your family isn't bribing me in any way, shape, or form." He set his hand on the car, next to her shoulder, nearly trapping her between the car and his body, although he still wasn't touching her.

"Then why?"

His gaze scanned her face, dipping to her lips. She had an insane urge to fish around for some Chapstick. Why was he looking at her lips?

"I don't think you want me to answer that," he said.

Evie's brows popped up. "Why not?"

He lifted his other hand and ran his thumb along her cheek, then tucked some of her blowing hair behind her ear. Did he realize that his touch was giving her all kinds of thoughts? He didn't drop his hand, but rested it on her shoulder. So now her heart was pounding, and her legs turning to water.

"I'll answer your question if you answer mine."

"Okay," she said, her voice a mere breath.

"Why haven't you ever been kissed?"

Evie blinked, then blinked again. His body wasn't pressed against hers, but she could feel the warmth of his body all the same. "It's not that guys haven't tried to kiss me, but we've always been interrupted, and then everything fizzled. Every time. Bad luck, I guess."

That crease between his brows appeared again. "Interrupted, how?"

He really wanted to know this? When she was about to melt on the spot?

"Um, my only date in high school was sort of a disaster from the start," she said. "I mean, we had fun as a group for senior prom. When Aaron dropped me off at my house, he walked me to the door. I knew he liked me, and I liked him, but my brothers had been cornering him all week at school and lecturing him. I could tell he was getting his courage up, and he grabbed my hands in his super sweaty ones. Just as he leaned in, my brothers opened the front door. Aaron jumped about a mile high and *ran* back to his truck. He never spoke to or even looked at me again."

Carson was smiling.

"It's not funny," Evie said, slapping his chest.

He caught her hand against his chest. "It's a little bit funny."

Evie made a face. "That's because it didn't happen to *you.*"

"What about your next almost-kiss?"

He was still holding her hand against his chest, and she could feel the warmth of his skin coming through his shirt. "My freshman year in college, I went out with a guy in my math class. He was geeky, but in a cute way."

Carson's fingers wrapped around her hand, securing her even closer.

"He tried to kiss me in his car, but someone literally ran into us," she said. "It was just a fender bender, but that kind of ruined the moment, and he never asked me out again."

Now, Carson was grinning.

"I see that I'm your night's entertainment," she said.

"You are," he said. "Who was your next victim?"

She tried to slap his chest again, but he held her hand firmly.

"Seth and I were on our second date," she said. "We'd gotten ice cream cones and were walking across campus. He stopped me near a tree, and just before he kissed me, the sky crackled with lightning. Then the rain came, pouring like we were in a tropical storm. We ran for cover, but all he could talk about was that he'd dropped his cell phone somewhere. So we spent the next twenty minutes searching for it in the rain and mud."

Carson chuckled. "Let me guess, he didn't call you."

"Nope," she said. Carson was so close that she could practically hear his heartbeat. Could *he* hear hers thumping away?

"Well, the way I see it, sweetness, is that your brothers are nowhere in sight," Carson drawled. "And we're not sitting in a car. And it's overcast, but no pending storm."

"The way you *see* it?" she asked. "What are you talking about?"

"I think I need to help you break your no-kissing streak." He moved his hand to cradle her face.

"Oh, really?" she whispered, her pulse racing like a mad horse.

"Really," he whispered back. "What do you think, sweetness?"

She swallowed. She inhaled, then exhaled. Her stomach felt like she was on the first turn of a rollercoaster. She only had to say one word, and everything would change. She let her eyelids flutter shut, then she said, "Yes."

Carson's hand slipped behind her neck, and his mouth found hers. His mouth was warm, and his lips soft. The scruff of his jaw scraped against her chin, sending tingles through her. *Carson was kissing her.* She was being kissed! For the first time. *Ever.* She should have frozen, but her imagination seemed to have dreamt of this moment for a very long time, and her arms wrapped around his neck, her heels lifted up, and her body pressed close.

She moved her mouth against his, mimicking his movements, trying to learn, trying to kiss him like he was kissing her. His hand that was braced against the car moved to her waist, and he drew her even closer as he continued to kiss her slowly. Taking his time. Sending bursts of heat through her.

It was hard to catch a full breath, but she didn't care. Her every sense was on alert as the curves of her body fit against the planes of his. Her fingers found his hair, and she dragged them through his softness. His hand moved up her back, skimming over her sweatshirt, then anchoring at the nape of her neck.

When he broke off their kiss and lifted his head, she opened her eyes to find him gazing at her.

"I think you're lying," he rasped.

Surprise zinged through her. "What?"

His eyes were as dark as the night, and his breathing was as rapid as hers. "You kiss like you know what you're doing."

His body was still pressed against hers, and she didn't want him to stop kissing her. Not for a long time. "Maybe I'm a natural."

A smiled formed on his face. Then he was kissing her again. This time, it wasn't slow and gentle and simmering. This time, he trapped her against the car, and tugged her hips against his. She opened her mouth to him, and he took it deeper, as if he'd been waiting for her permission. Well, he had it.

She had to clutch his shirt to hang on, because she was pretty sure her feet weren't touching the ground. And she was also pretty sure she wouldn't ever release him. Carson's mouth on hers was an ambrosia she could have never imagined or dreamed up. Was it him? Or was all kissing like this?

A light blared to her right, and it took her a second to

realize that the porch light had turned on. Was Carson's grandpa . . .

Carson didn't release her, though. He seemed to be completely oblivious to the screen door creaking open and his grandpa's voice calling out, "Carson, you out there? You didn't lock up."

Evie didn't know whether to laugh or be mortified. Carson hadn't moved, hadn't released her, although now he was resting his forehead against hers. Grinning at her.

"Your grandpa's on the porch," she whispered.

"I know," Carson said. "Give him a minute, he'll go away."

"I can hear you, Carson," his grandpa said. "Where are you?"

Then, a flashlight shone in their faces.

Carson turned, holding up his hand against the glare. "Pops! Turn it off!"

"Oh, you *are* out here," his grandpa said. "I wasn't sure."

"Turn it off," Carson demanded again, and the flashlight flicked off.

Evie thought she heard a chuckle from the old man.

"Good night, Evie," Mr. Hunt said before going back inside and letting the screen door snap closed behind him.

"Good night, Mr. Hunt," Evie said in a tremulous tone.

Carson pulled her close again, his hands sliding over her shoulders.

"Sorry about that," he rumbled.

"I did warn you that kissing me was a hazard."

Carson smiled. "You did. But I think we got plenty of kissing in before we were interrupted, so I consider that progress."

Evie knew what was coming next. He'd release her, and she'd get in the car and drive back home. Then she'd lay awake reliving it all again and again. And tomorrow? What? Would she and Carson hang out? Kiss again? Avoid each other? She was so lost.

"You're thinking too hard," he said, his tone teasing. "Stop biting your lip. It just makes me want to kiss you again."

Evie smirked, and Carson kissed her anyway. It was a soft kiss, a lingering kiss, like he was reluctant to release her.

When he finally did pull away, she had to ask. "Carson . . . ?"

"Hmm?"

"Why did you kiss me?"

His eyes crinkled at the corners. "Are you sure you want to know?"

What kind of question was that? She nodded.

Carson traced a lazy circle along her neck with his thumb. "Because I like you, Evie Prosper," he said, "and I've been thinking about kissing you for a while."

"My family—"

His fingers covered her mouth. "Stop. This isn't about your family." He moved his fingers and kissed the edge of her mouth. Then he kissed lower, just beneath her jaw. "You're ruining the mood when you talk about your family while I'm trying to kiss you."

She could feel his smile against her neck.

"Don't blame *my* family," she said. "It was *your* grandpa who shined a flashlight in our eyes."

He chuckled, then continued his exploration of her neck.

Evie was on fire, absolutely going up in flames. She slipped her hands into his hair and closed her eyes as waves of sensation crashed through her. When his lips grazed her collarbone, she knew she had to tell him good night, or her brain would be completely scrambled.

"Carson, I should go."

His arms tightened about her for a moment as he inhaled, then he lifted his head.

She met his gaze with a half-smile. "Thanks for breaking my no-kissing record."

His brows quirked. "Really? Is that what's happening?"

"You said so yourself."

"Yeah, well . . ." his voice trailed off as he ran his fingers along her braid. "This is not a one-time thing, so you'd better not ghost me."

Evie's heart might have fluttered. "You know where to find me. Or my brothers."

"Hmm." His gaze was on her, his eyes half-slitted. "What time do you get up? Maybe we can get breakfast at that diner."

She stared at him. Going out in public with Carson, especially if he did any sort of PDA, would pretty much announce to the entire world that they were . . . together. Did one kiss—okay, a lot of kissing in one night—make them a couple? *Were* they a couple? Would it be lame to ask? To show how clueless she felt?

"You can say no," Carson said, his brow wrinkling as he stepped away, leaving a gap of cool air between them. "I mean, if it takes you this long to decide, then I think I know the answer."

"Wait," she said, grasping his arm. "I mean, yes, I'll go to breakfast with you. Is this like a date?"

His gaze searched hers for a moment. "Yes, ma'am. That is, if it's okay with you."

"Seven-thirty, then. After the ranch hands get their breakfast, so it's not too crowded."

Carson tipped an imaginary hat. "All right, then. I'll be the guy on your front porch at 7:30 in the morning."

Her heart was about to burst at the sight of this beautiful

man in the moonlight, telling her he'd be picking her up for breakfast in a handful of hours. "Okay."

"Okay?"

She nodded, a smile spreading on her face.

"Good." He reached around her and opened her door.

But before she could slide past him, he lifted his hand to her jaw to anchor her in place. He kissed her again, chastely, but he lingered, and her eyes floated shut.

"Good night," he whispered.

"Good night," she whispered back.

14

CARSON HUNT WAS IN trouble. His grandad stood in his bedroom doorway before the crack of dawn. Hands on his skinny hips, cowboy boots caked in mud, and his shirt sopping wet. It had rained during the night, but Carson hadn't minded. In fact, he liked the patter of rain while he thought about the delicious kiss, or multiple kisses, with Evie.

She'd been perfect. Too perfect. And that's why he was in trouble.

Whatever Grandad wanted could be fixed, Carson was sure of it.

But, Evie? That was much more complicated.

"What's going on?" Carson asked, sitting up in bed and scrubbing at his hair.

"The garden's completely flooded, and everything we planted yesterday is washed out."

"That's not good." Carson reached for a shirt and slipped it on. Then he snatched his jeans. Next came on his boots. "Can anything be salvaged?"

"I don't know," Grandad said.

It wasn't like Grandad to be so dejected by a few washed-out plants. Yeah, the work would have to be redone, but as Carson passed by him, he slowed.

"Everything okay, Pops?" he asked.

Grandad folded his arms. "What are your intentions with Evie Prosper?"

This stopped Carson cold. He eyed his grandad. "We're spending a little time together."

"I got that," Grandad said. "Seeing the two of you lip-locked last night made that loud and clear. But that woman isn't someone you can date, then drop later. She's pure-blood around here, and if I know any of the Prosper men, they'll have your hide for 'spending a little time' with her."

Carson frowned. "She's twenty-two, and we didn't do anything more than—"

Grandad raised a hand. "You don't need to explain to me, son; I'm just telling you how it is."

With a sigh, Carson folded his arms and leaned against the wall in the hallway. "She told me about her brothers and how they'd grill guys who were interested in her. She didn't even really date until she went to college because of that." He wasn't going to tell his grandad that last night had been her first kiss ever. That might make this all into a bigger deal.

"I'm not surprised," Grandad said. "Those men are protective of their own. They aren't going to stand by while some dude takes advantage of their sister."

Carson's stomach clenched. "I'm not taking advantage of her. She's an amazing woman, and I think she likes me, too." Well, he *knew* she liked him, even if she didn't want to fully admit she might like a small-town cowboy.

"I know you'd never take advantage of a woman," Grandad said. "You haven't even dated since Stacee, and I'm glad you're starting to live beyond school and work now. Seeing that there's a life out there to be had. And Evie Prosper seems like a good woman all the way around. She's young, in my opinion, but everyone seems young to me nowadays."

Carson waited for his grandad to drop the bomb, and here it came . . .

"But unless you are dating Evie Prosper for keeps, you'd better steer clear of her," Grandad said. "I plan on retiring here and living out the rest of my life. I don't want a neighborly feud because my grandson messed around with the mayor's daughter."

Carson's mouth opened, then shut. He shook his head, hardly believing his grandad was basically giving him two choices. He felt like he'd just met Evie, yet also felt like he knew her better than anyone he'd ever dated, including Stacee. Evie wore her heart on her sleeve, she was vulnerable, she was sweet, she was adorable, and Carson wanted to see her every minute of the day.

He didn't know the future, especially with Evie not interested in living in Prosper. Unless . . . he had some power to convince her. But right now, he couldn't make any promises, and his grandad had to know that.

"I won't do anything to embarrass you or piss off the Prosper family," Carson said, clasping a hand on his shoulder. "Now, let me see what the damage is. I've got a breakfast appointment in an hour, and when the ground is dry enough, I'll put the garden to rights."

His grandad grumbled, but there was a lighter step to his stride as Carson followed him down the hallway.

"Am I invited to this breakfast appointment?" Grandad asked over his shoulder.

"I'll bring you back a box of food, how does that sound?"

Grandad chuckled. "You're a stubborn boy, you know that?"

They'd reached the back door, and Carson looked over at

his grandad, the man who'd sacrificed so much to provide for his two grandsons. "I'm not going to be breaking anyone's heart," Carson said. "I've had enough of that in my life already."

Grandad lifted his chin. "I trust you, son, always have."

With a lump in his throat, Carson opened the back door and walked out onto the patio. Yep, Pops had been right. The garden was completely washed out. He walked to the edge of the scrubby grass, not getting into the mud just yet. There would be time for that later.

"I'll stop by the feed store and pick out more starters," Carson told his grandad, who'd come to join him. "Maybe we should set up a tarp? Are we expecting more downpours like this?"

"Nah," Grandad said, rubbing the back of his sunburned neck. Then he lit a cigarette. "This, from what I hear, doesn't happen too often. And when you get back, we've got to sketch out where we want the corrals."

"You've decided to accept Holt Prosper's offer?"

"I have."

So the two families would be in business together. As Carson washed up before going over to Prosperity Ranch, he wished he didn't feel like time was running out. Both he and Evie graduated next month, and both would be making lifelong decisions.

Though he'd been here only a few days, Carson already knew he'd be moving to Prosper. For how long, he didn't know. But at least initially. Grandad needed help, and Carson would never be able to pay back what Grandad had done for him, but he could at least try. Whether that meant staying beyond the few months it would take to get the house in decent shape and help with building the corrals, he didn't know.

By the time he reached Prosperity Ranch and walked up the steps of the front porch, the sun had already cleared the horizon, and the cool morning air felt good on Carson's perspiring neck. Yeah, he was nervous for some reason. Probably because he wasn't sure how Evie would react to him. They'd crossed a pretty major line last night, and if Carson had his way, their relationship would keep progressing. But what did Evie think?

He was about to knock softly when the door opened, and Evie stepped out. She wasn't wearing the baggy sweatshirt and shorts of last night, or the jeans of earlier in that day—she wore a pretty sundress. It reminded him of the first night he saw her. Her hair was down in long waves, and the patterned green sundress skimmed the tops of her knees.

She turned and shut the door behind her, then tugged on a denim jacket over her bare shoulders. Carson stepped close to help her slide into it.

"Thank you," she said, glancing up at him.

He saw the vulnerability and wariness in her blue eyes.

"Good morning," he said.

Her lips curved. "Good morning."

Then, he leaned down and kissed her. A soft, brief, totally unplanned kiss. He didn't know if she was surprised, but he was stunned himself. It seemed the moment he saw her, something inside of him had caved.

He lifted his head and found her eyes on him.

"Well, Carson Hunt, you're definitely not a shy man."

"Never have been."

She turned, a half-smile on her face, and walked down the steps.

Carson watched her for a moment, then caught up and opened the passenger door. He placed his hand on her elbow as she climbed into the truck. She didn't say anything, but clipped on her seatbelt. So he shut the door and walked around the front of the truck. When he climbed in and started it, he glanced over at her. "You look beautiful this morning."

"So do you," she said, her cheeks flushing a pretty pink. "I mean, handsome or whatever you want to call it."

He smiled as he pulled out of the driveway, then reached for her hand, and her fingers slipped easily through his. Warm and smooth. It was nice—very nice. "You can call me whatever you want, sweetness."

"Are you always like this with the ladies?"

He glanced over at her before pulling onto the main road. Her gaze was teasing, but he knew the question was leading. "You're the only lady I'm with."

She raised a brow. "Is that also what you tell all the ladies?"

He ran his thumb over her knuckles. "I haven't dated since I broke up with my girlfriend two years ago."

He felt the shift in the air from her surprise, and her curiosity. He should probably explain, because he needed to tell her some things. Things that the woman he was dating should know, and he sure hoped they were dating. But they were nearly to the diner. He pulled into the angled parking spot in front of the restaurant and shut off the engine. Instead of letting go of her hand, he said, "Two years ago, my older brother, Rhett, was killed in a motorcycle accident. A lot of things changed after that, including my relationship with my girlfriend, Stacee."

Evie stayed silent, gazing at their clasped hands.

"I went through a rough patch," he said. "Didn't really talk to anyone for a while. Maybe it was depression or something, or long-term grief. Basically, my friends stopped coming around eventually. Stacee gave up. My grandad was virtually the only one I talked to for months. Him and my coaches, if only absolutely necessary. Otherwise, I kept my head down, did my workouts on the team, played the games, went to classes, and avoided all social interaction."

Evie shifted in her seat and faced him. She placed her other hand on his forearm. "I'm sorry about your brother," she said. "I don't even know what to say."

"You don't have to say anything," Carson said. "No one knows what to say. That's just it. I'm working through this on my own time. Yeah, it's taking a while, but I can't go at anyone else's pace."

Evie moved her hand up his arm, slowly caressing his skin. "Don't worry about anyone else, then. You do what you have to do."

He nodded. "I have been. That's why I decided to continue with my education at another school. I couldn't face all the guys on my team anymore. I needed a fresh start, but I wasn't ready to face the real world, either. Grandad's offer is a major blessing in my life, like he's always been."

Evie was watching him closely, and yes, there was compassion and sympathy in her eyes. Something he'd seen dozens of times in his former friends' eyes. But with Evie, it didn't bother him. It didn't weigh him down with more responsibility to get over the death of his brother and be back to his old self again.

"What was he like?"

"Rhett?"

She nodded.

Carson exhaled. "He was good at everything, A showman, or a showoff, I guess. But I had more discipline, so I ended up getting the athletic scholarship. He came to all my games. Both he and Grandad. They were both my number-one support."

"And your parents?"

"My mom took off soon after I was born. I haven't seen my dad since I was thirteen."

Her fingers tightened on his. "Your grandad's a good man."

"The best."

She looked up at him then, and in her eyes, he saw a spark of something. More than compassion. Understanding? "I think you'll grow to love Prosper, Carson. You can find a home here. People who you can care about and not have to try to be someone you aren't."

"I don't know about Prosper ever being a true home," he said in a soft voice.

One of her eyebrows arched. "Give it time."

He lifted his other hand to cup her cheek. "I'm trying to, but without you in Prosper, I can't make any guarantees."

Her eyes widened, and maybe he'd been too bold and open, but when he leaned down and gently kissed her, she still kissed him back. So he decided he'd take that small victory. When he reluctantly drew away, she said, "Carson, you know what I've already decided."

He brushed his fingers along her neck, then drew one of her wavy locks forward. "I know, but can you blame a man for trying?"

15

CARSON HUNT WAS MESMERIZING. That was the only way Evie could explain it. The fact that he hadn't dated for the past two years had astounded her. And the fact that he'd lost his older brother in a tragic accident was heartbreaking.

This man had past sorrows that she couldn't even begin to comprehend, yet, here he was in a tiny town in Texas, helping out his grandad. Even though Carson would soon earn a prestigious master's degree, he was set on helping his grandad with his business of restoring rodeo grounds, which amounted to a lot of paperwork and tons of manual labor.

As they ate at the diner—Evie having chosen the two-scrambled-egg plate, and Carson the same thing, but adding on a stack of hot cakes—she barely noticed anyone else in the restaurant. Oh, she'd said hi to folks, but she'd been anxious to return her focus to Carson. Because he was practically all she could think about anyway, and this was their first official date, right?

"Tell me why you decided to go into graphic design," Carson asked, after finishing off his orange juice.

Evie shrugged. Normally, she told people it was because graphic design was less risky than other types of art. One could always make a living at it. But after Carson had bared his soul to her, she didn't want to give him her generic answer. "When I was a kid, I used to spend hours at the library going through news websites. I was fascinated by news, but mostly I was fascinated by the website layouts. I know, it's totally geeky."

Carson's eyes were warm as he listened. "It's not geeky. I'd love to see your stuff."

Evie shrugged. "Well, maybe you'll get lucky, because they're amazing."

He chuckled, and she was glad he knew she was kidding.

"I just wish I could figure out something that will set me above the other interviewees."

Carson nodded. "What if you bring graphic design samples, you know, of your ideas to improve the newspaper's website."

Evie blinked. "That's a really good idea."

"Unless it would take too much time."

"I could just do one or two samples," she said. "It would give them an idea of what I can do that's directly related to them."

"Exactly." Carson smiled, and she smiled back.

"I thought that was you," a woman said, her voice sing-songing above Evie.

She looked up to see Barb. They'd never been friends because the two-year age gap had seemed too great back in school. Plus, Evie was hardly the popular girl in school. More like the person everyone avoided, unless they were trying to get to one of her brothers. Barb was dressed to the nines, as usual. Her blonde hair was pulled into a high ponytail, and she looked like she could step into an arena and take first place in barrel-racing by appearance alone. Her white jeans were studded with sequins on the seams, and her orange and white shirt reminded Evie of a Creamsicle ice cream bar.

Her silver earrings bobbed, and her silver bracelets jangled as she propped a hand on her hip. "Evie Prosper, it's been a day and a year since I saw you. Now, look at you, you're all grown up."

Evie smiled, although she only felt annoyed at the interruption. She rose from her chair and gave Barb a quick hug. A cloud of perfume seemed to hover around the woman.

When Evie pulled away, Barb's gaze had already lasered to Carson.

"Who's this, sugar?" Barb extended her hand, her fake nails gleaming in the diner's overhead light.

"Carson, this is Barbie, our neighbor on the opposite side," Evie said, not missing how Barb was thoroughly checking him out. "Barb, this is Carson Hunt."

"Oh!" Barb said, her mouth making a comical O. "You're Mr. Hunt's grandson! He told me y'all were coming this week. I'd planned to bring over a cherry pie. Do you like cherries, sugar?"

Evie was more than annoyed now. The words Barb was speaking were friendly, even neighborly, but her tone of voice was full of all kinds of insinuations.

"I like cherries just fine," Carson said. "I'm sure my grandad would enjoy a pie."

Barb rested a hand on Carson's shoulder. "You don't like pie?"

His voice was more stiff when he said, "I'm never opposed to pie, ma'am."

"Oh, don't *ma'am* me," she said. "If I'm older than you, it's not by much. Besides, we're practically neighbors. I'm only a short hop past Prosperity Ranch." Her eyes fluttered as she moved close to Carson. "Y'all coming to the battle of the bands tonight at Racoons?"

Carson actually looked interested, but Evie held back a

groan. The name 'battle of the bands' was a huge exaggeration. A couple of cowboys strumming their guitars at the town bar. It wasn't much of a battle, and there weren't any actual bands.

And . . . Barb's hand was still on Carson's shoulder.

He looked directly at Evie. "I don't know. I'll have to ask Evie. What are our plans, sweetness?"

Carson had called her sweetness from day one, and Evie knew enough to not get hot and bothered over it. But when he said it this time, the meaning was clear. Barb stepped away from them. "Are y'all *dating*? Oh, how adorable! That's just precious." Her smile broadened. "I know your mamma has wanted you to settle in Prosper. Oh, this is just perfect!"

Evie cringed, because if Barb said anything to her mother . . . which she would in about five hot minutes.

"Don't get ahead of yourself, Barbie," she shot out, maybe too firmly. "I haven't made any decisions yet. So please don't get my mom's hopes up."

Barb's eyebrows skyrocketed. "Oh, I see. You're gonna surprise her. I don't blame you. This man of yours is yummy. Um-hm." She winked at Carson, then said to Evie, "I'll be as silent as a water skeeter. No one will hear a word from me. I won't even tell Patsy and Jana. They'll be at Racoons, too, but they won't hear it from me!"

Then she was gone.

Sashaying out the door, leaving an open-mouthed Evie in her wake, and probably a confused Carson. Patsy and Jana? Patsy was older than Evie, but Jana was one of those girls her age who made Cruella Deville look nice. The last thing she wanted to do was run into Jana—even if she'd matured or somehow grown a heart.

"I've got to get home," Evie said, jumping to her feet. "Barb is probably going to have my mom cornered in two seconds flat."

She was nearly to the door when Carson caught up with her. "Easy, I still need to pay."

Evie stopped. "Okay. You pay, and I'll wait in the truck."

Carson looked like he was about to argue, but then he opened the door for her. She hurried out of the diner, pulling out her phone. Then she saw the time. It was only 8:30 a.m. Would Barb knock on the door this early?

It wasn't that Evie couldn't clear up the misconception, but now she and Carson would be completely exposed, and she didn't know if she wanted that. This was new territory for her. They'd kissed, and flirted, and kissed some more. And they were on a date.

Well, Evie would be answering questions from her family, and they'd just have to live with it. Plus, it wasn't like she was falling in love with Carson Hunt or anything. She wasn't going to get her heart broken, and she wasn't going to move back to Prosper for anyone.

The driver's door popped open, and Carson climbed in.

"Sorry about that," Evie said. "Barb gets under my skin." She didn't bother to get into the whole thing about Jana and Patsy. Barb was enough of an explanation.

He didn't look exactly convinced, but he started the truck and pulled onto Main Street.

"She used to obsess over Holt. Well, both Knox and Holt," Evie clarified. "Barb's like a gnat that won't go away." She eyed Carson, his eyes forward on the road, the easy way he maneuvered his truck. "Did you think she was pretty?"

Carson shot her a look, then said, "She seems like an entertaining person, and yeah, she's pretty."

Evie's gut squeezed. She could see it now. Carson would come back to Prosper after graduation, and Barb would forget all about her previous crushes, and zero in on him. Otherwise, Carson would have his pick of women in the town. Evie looked out her window, her eyes stinging. Just because she'd finally had her first kiss didn't mean she owned the man, or that he had to be loyal to her.

"What are you doing?" she asked as the truck slowed and stopped on the side of the road.

"Come here."

She turned to look at him. His left arm was draped over the steering wheel, and he'd extended his right hand.

"What for?"

"You're too far away." Carson tugged her hand toward him, and she scooted closer.

"That's better," he whispered. Then he leaned down, and his mouth covered hers, slow and sweet. She'd kissed him more than once by now, but this kiss . . . this one left no doubt that she was the only woman on his mind. He pulled her close as he continued to explore her mouth, and yep, she melted. She wrapped her arms about his neck, and his hands settled at her waist.

Kissing Carson made it hard to remember why she was in such a hurry to get back home. She was fine right here, in his arms, her skin buzzing at his touch.

"Carson," she whispered as she drew away so she could catch her breath. "Are you trying to distract me?"

"Mmm," he rumbled, his dark eyes a slit as he studied her. "Is it working?"

"Yes," she said.

The edge of his mouth lifted. "You're a beautiful woman, Evie Prosper. Don't ever think that Barb holds a candle to you. I don't like fake, never have."

Evie moved her hands over his shoulder, then down his chest, appreciating the hard planes of his muscles. "I don't like fake, either."

"Good, then we're on the same page." His lips found her

neck, and like last night, her pulse skyrocketed. The scruff of his chin tickled, and she couldn't help but laugh.

"Someone's gonna pull over and see if we need help," she said.

"Then you can introduce me." He lifted his head to gaze at her with amusement. "As your date."

This sobered her. "You know my family, they're going to make a big deal out of this."

Carson seemed to sober, too, but he didn't pull away, didn't release her. "Yeah, my grandad warned me."

Evie frowned. "Really?"

Carson released a sigh as his fingers trailed along her arm, then linked with her hand. He brought her hand to his lips and pressed a kiss there. "He doesn't want anything that happens between us to affect the relationship between our families. Reminded me that your dad is the mayor, and—"

Evie put two fingers to his lips. "Stop. I know it all. I've grown up with it. My great-grandparents settled this town. My dad's the mayor. My brother Knox a rodeo legend." Her eyes burned, and her voice trembled. "And apparently, I can't have a life, date anyone, or have a boyfriend without everyone putting in their two bits and telling me what to do."

"Hey," Carson said in a whisper, pulling her close.

"I'm twenty-two, Carson," Evie said. "I had my first kiss *last night*. And I can't be under everyone's thumb all the time." She drew away from him, even though it was the last thing she wanted to do. "You're amazing, and you listen to me, and I have a huge crush on you, but maybe . . . maybe we need to end this now before it gets farther down the road. Dating you is just going to bring out the panic in everyone, for whatever reason, starting with your grandad. He's a great guy, and I have nothing against him, but if he's already worried—"

"Evie," Carson said, running a thumb over her cheek

because her tears had started. "Ignore them all. I'm going to. We can date if we want to. Casually. No expectations. No promises. You can call things off whenever you want. No hard feelings. It will be good for your family to see you making your own decisions about a guy. We don't even have to talk about your family if you don't want to."

"We're in Prosper."

His smile was slow. "Yeah, but not for long."

"True."

His fingers moved to her jawline, still caressing, still warm.

Evie closed her eyes at his touch. "What happens when we get back to San Antonio?"

"I don't know," he said. "We'll take it a day at a time, okay?"

She opened her eyes to find his dark ones on her. "Okay."

"And I wouldn't mind if you want to keep kissing me," he said, smiling now.

She moved closer again, and leaned her head against his shoulder. She wrapped her arms tightly about him, and he wrapped her up in warmth and steadiness. The last thing she wanted to do was hurt Carson, or use him, and she couldn't make any promises. But if he didn't need any, then she'd be happy to take things one day at a time.

16

CARSON HAD LIED—MAYBE not to Evie, but to himself. He did have hope for something more. Desired it. With his whole heart, in fact. He wanted her to move back to Prosper. Maybe she just needed to live somewhere other than her family ranch? Were there apartments or rooms for rent in town? He hadn't seen any apartment or condo complexes.

He also knew that he was moving way too fast in his head. Who would have thought a couple of weeks ago that he'd meet a woman and feel so strongly about her? It was like his heart had been waiting for the right woman. Was it possible that he already knew she was the right one? Problem was, she was struggling with the whole Prosper thing.

It was one thing to declare she wasn't moving back home to her small town, but it was another to see how upset she was around her family, even though she loved them dearly. Carson knew it wasn't his place to confront her brothers, or even her father, about what she was feeling and going through. Plus, Evie would probably resent him for interfering.

He did stand by what he told her. She needed to own her decisions about who she dated and when. Which happened to be him, but in general, it seemed that Evie hadn't really stood up for herself in the past. That day when she'd come flying out of the house to chew out her brothers was probably the first time.

"You got the supplies?" Grandad's voice rang out from the front porch, where he was stubbing out a cigarette. "Or are you just woolgathering?"

Carson climbed out of the truck. "Both." He'd taken Evie home, then driven back to the feed store to replenish the washed-out starter plants for the garden.

Grandad walked toward the truck, and Carson met him at the back. He lowered the door to the bed of the truck.

"What in the Sam is all this?" Grandad pointed at the paving stones.

"I'm going to surround the garden with them," Carson said. "Give it more shape. I looked up a few ideas online."

"We don't need to be fancy."

Carson smiled. "Not intending to be fancy. Just trying to prevent another complete loss if it rains before these new plants take root."

"All right, then," Grandad said, picking up one of the flats of small potted plants.

Carson lifted four paving stones and walked with Grandad around the house to the garden. The sun was starting to dry out the land, but it would be hours yet.

He began situating the paving stones while his grandad finished bringing the plants.

"How was your date with Evie Prosper?" Grandad asked after a moment, setting his hands on his hips as he watched.

Carson looked over at him. "She's an amazing woman, and we're dating. If I have to answer to the Prosper family, I will."

Grandad's jaw tightened. "You've made up your mind?"

Carson straightened and met his grandad's gaze full on. "I have."

His grandad held his gaze for a moment, then he nodded. "I'll be inside making a few phone calls to builders about getting a quote for the corrals. Let me know if you need anything."

Carson nodded. Once his grandad had disappeared into the house, Carson brushed off his hands and pulled his phone from his pocket. He sent Evie a text, but when she didn't reply soon, he pocketed his phone again. He wondered how talking to her mom or even her family was going. She'd told him that she'd have to preempt any gossip that Barb would spread.

Two hours later, Carson finished up with replanting the garden. The midday sun was great for the ground, but he was half-drenched in both mud and sweat.

"Got a visitor," Grandad said after pushing open the back door.

Carson turned and shielded his eyes from the sun, hoping that it might be Evie. Although, she probably would have walked around the house. Nope. Holt Prosper's tall form stepped out of the house behind Grandad.

"How are you doing, Holt?" Carson said as the guy approached.

Holt had his cowboy hat pushed back on his head, and the dirt on his pants told Carson that he'd been hard at work on something.

"I've been better," Holt said, his brows drawn together.

Carson brushed dirt from his hands, but it didn't do much good. He glanced at his grandad, who was wearing his poker face.

"Is there something I can help you with?" Carson continued, ignoring the knot tightening in his stomach. This had to be about Evie . . .

"There is." Holt nodded at Grandad, who turned and headed back to the house.

"Wanna sit down?" Carson motioned toward the chairs on the back patio.

"This'll take but a minute," Holt said. "Evie told us that the two of you are dating."

Carson lifted his chin. "We are."

"When you arrived, giving our sister a lift to Prosper, we were told that things were platonic between the two of you."

"Also correct," Carson said.

Holt folded his arms, and for a long moment, he said nothing, but eyed Carson. "Evie's not the typical girl. She doesn't always make the smartest decisions. She's naïve about a lot of things."

Carson waited, not sure where Holt was going with all of this. What did any of it have to do with dating him?

"As the mayor's daughter, she's gotten a lot of attention over the years from guys," Holt continued. "Their intentions haven't been upstanding. They think an in with the mayor's daughter is an in with the mayor himself."

"So that they could get permission to expand a store on Main Street or something?" Carson asked.

Holt frowned. "No—"

"Are men trying to date Evie so they can get a sure bid into the rodeo? Or maybe they want to bribe her to ask her daddy if they can get funding for a Fourth of July parade float?"

"Now, see here—"

"No, *you* see here." Carson took a step forward. "Prosper is a small town, and I understand that to the Prosper family, it's everything. The sun rises and sets with the Prosper family around here. But about five miles away from here is another town, and beyond that another town, then an entire state, then an entire country. Do you really think that your sister of all people doesn't know that there is an entirely different world out there?"

Holt's eyes were narrowed, but he was listening.

"You say that your sister isn't the typical girl. But I disagree. She's a grown woman, and you need to stop treating her like a kid." He held up a hand to stop whatever Holt was about to say. "You say she doesn't make smart decisions, but that's not true. You don't *allow* her to make any decisions, so how is she supposed to learn to make smart ones? And she's not naïve about anything. She's hurt. By her own family's lack of trust and faith in her."

Holt's jaw clenched as he narrowed his blue eyes at Carson. "You finished?"

Carson took another step. "Not quite. Evie is a woman with her own mind. She's nearly a college graduate, and she's done most things in life to make you and your family happy. What about what makes *her* happy? Have you ever considered that?"

Holt chuckled, but it wasn't a friendly chuckle. "Are you implying that *you* now meet that criteria?"

Carson scoffed. "Not at all. I'm just happy to spend time with her, if she wants to, but it's all her decision. It will always be her decision. She'll figure out what she wants in life soon enough—where she wants to live, and who she wants to be with. She doesn't need interference and loud opinions from her family."

"What does she need?" Holt asked in a skeptical tone.

"Faith and support," Carson said. "A little trust goes a long way, too."

Holt rubbed his neck, his gaze still steady on him. "I can't disagree with that."

Carson nodded. He counted this as progress.

"But what I want to know," Holt continued, "is what are your intentions with my sister?"

Carson had no problem answering that. "My intentions

are to take things one day at a time. She's in the saddle, and she's holding the reins. I'm not going to put any of my ambitions ahead of hers. She knows that if I relocate to Prosper after graduation, that will probably be a deal-breaker. So, you could say right now, that things are casual between us. Neither of us is looking at things permanently."

Holt was still frowning. "You playing her?"

"No, sir," Carson said. "She's an amazing woman who I hope to all that is holy will change her mind about this small town your family worships so much. But I'll never force her into a decision, or make her feel guilty about what she chooses for herself."

Holt looked away for a moment and sighed. "What about you?"

"Me?"

Holt met his gaze again. "Yeah, you. Your grandad told us about your brother, and some of the stuff you went through. Do you think you're setting yourself up for more heartbreak?"

Carson didn't miss the sincerity of Holt's tone, which shifted the entire mood of their conversation. He looked down at the dirt on his hands and absently brushed at them. "I'm not gonna lie, Holt. It's a possibility." He met the man's gaze again. "Whatever happens, it's a privilege to be friends with your sister. And if she never returns to Prosper, well, there will definitely be a hole in my heart."

Holt eyed him. "Yet, you're not going to influence her decision in whether to move back?"

"Not unless it's just my good looks and charm that convince her."

Holt laughed, and Carson couldn't have been more relieved.

Then, to his astonishment, the Prosper brother stuck out his hand.

Carson gripped Holt's hand, and the two men shook.

"All I'm gonna say is that my sister's a spitfire," Holt said, "but if you break her heart, you'll have me and half the town to answer to."

Carson swallowed, both pride and humility burning in his chest. "Yes, sir."

As Holt headed off the property, Carson didn't move for several moments, reviewing the conversation in his mind. Things had gone well, right? It was almost like he had permission from Holt to date his sister. Not that he needed it, and not that Evie needed permission, either.

Yet . . . he felt lighter. He felt amazing. If he wasn't so dirty and sweaty, he'd head over to Prosperity Ranch right now and talk to Evie. Gingerly, he pulled out his phone from his pocket. Still no reply from her.

Carson trudged to the back patio and tugged off his boots. Inside, he found Grandad with the TV blaring, but he muted it as soon as Carson stepped in.

"So?" Grandad said.

"I didn't back down, and he shook my hand," Carson said.

Grandad nodded, then unmuted the TV.

So . . . conversation over. By the time Carson got out of the shower, he was more impatient than ever about Evie not texting him back. Had Holt returned and reported? Was she even at the ranch?

He sat on the edge of his bed and called her number, unable to calm the thumping of his heart. Grandad still had the TV blaring, and was likely taking one of his covert naps he claimed to never need. Relief zinged through Carson when Evie answered.

"Hello?"

"Hey," he said.

"Hey."

He'd been fully prepared to ask her if she'd talked to her mom, or even if she knew about Holt coming over, but instead he said, "Wanna go on a picnic?"

"What? Are you serious?" The laughter in her tone was plain, but he only smiled.

Carson had no idea where the suggestion had come from, but now that he thought about it, it would be the perfect getaway from her family, the town's eyes, and his grandad.

"Yeah, I'm serious," he said, still smiling. "Don't I sound serious?"

"I guess." She laughed.

His body warmed at her sweet laughter.

"Where?"

"I don't know," he said. "You choose. I'll bring the picnic, and you tell me where to drive."

"Carson . . . do you even have a picnic basket?"

"Do we need one?" he said, then backtracked. "I'm sure there's one around here somewhere, or I can grab one."

"Okay, give me an hour."

Carson grinned as he hung up. He was going to need every minute of that hour to put together a picnic.

17

EVIE RESTED HER ARMS on the arena fence as she waited for Holt to come talk to her. She knew he'd gone to the Hunts', and when he returned, he said he needed to talk to her, but he had to get through a couple of phone calls first.

So, here she waited in the partial shade. Carson would be arriving in about thirty minutes, and she hoped whatever Holt wanted to talk to her about would be cleared up by then.

Her mom had just barely awakened when Evie had returned that morning. She'd told her mom, matter-of-factly, that she'd been on a breakfast date with Carson. Her mom had only smiled. "Good for you, Evie. He's a nice man."

That was it?

Evie had finally texted Becca to tell her that she'd been kissed. Then she spent the next twenty minutes texting back and forth with her friend. And an email had arrived on her phone. Evie had stared at the subject line for a long moment before opening it and reading it through.

She'd been asked for an interview at the *San Antonio Daily News*. A major publication, and one on her top five list. And the email wasn't a standard reply, either. The marketing directors referred to Evie's resume multiple times.

Oh boy. Evie's mind had started spinning in all directions. This was good—very, very good. Right? But the only thing she could think of was how her mom would react . . . and Carson. What would he do?

Evie had replied to the email and set up an interview time for the day after spring break ended. She didn't know how things would work with Carson once they were back at school. They'd take things one day at a time, though. That was all she could hold onto right now. Regardless, she had to tell her brothers that she was dating Carson.

Either that, or one of them would find out through the Barb gossip chain.

So, her heart thumping, she'd gone to the barn to find Holt and tell him the same thing.

Holt hadn't been so easy-going. In fact, he'd drilled her with quite a few questions, then he strode off.

Sometime later, he'd gotten in his truck and left. Evie had sensed her brother was going to talk to Carson.

What had Holt said to him? By his phone call, it appeared that whatever had been said between the two men, Carson hadn't been scared off.

And that thought made a horde of butterflies zing through her body.

"Sorry for the wait," Holt said, and Evie turned to see him approach.

He joined her at the railing. She could tell he was biding his time, trying to decide how to tell her what he'd come to talk to her about, as he gazed out over the arena.

"Had a talk with Carson Hunt."

Evie held her breath. Was she about to defend her choice of men she wanted to date?

"Well, I had a talk with him, and then he had a talk with *me.*"

Evie studied her brother, her pulse racing. "What do you mean?"

Holt turned to face her fully. He took off his cowboy hat and ran his hand through his brown hair. "Seems there's been a misunderstanding between us, Evie, and I apologize for that."

Then, her brother proceeded to tell her what Carson had said to him. How Carson had told Holt that the family needed to trust Evie and have more faith in her.

Evie could only stare at her brother as he repeated the conversation with Carson. At the end of it all, she still had no words.

Holt placed a hand on her shoulder. "I believe in you, and I trust you, sis," he said. "You've made the entire family proud, and I hope you can forgive my blockheadedness. I'll let Lane and Knox speak for themselves. But as far as I'm concerned, Carson Hunt is a good man, and even though you don't need my permission or anyone else's, I'm in your corner."

Evie blinked back the stinging tears, then she stepped forward into her brother's arms.

Holt held her tight.

"What's goin' on here?" her dad asked as he walked toward them.

Evie pulled away. "I'll let Holt tell you. I have a date to get ready for."

And without any other word of explanation, she ran toward the house, her heart thumping with gratitude and awe. She wished she could have been a witness to Carson and Holt's conversation. Had he really said all that stuff about her? Stood up for her?

She hurried into the house, calling out to her mom, "I'm going on a picnic with Carson."

Her mom said something, but Evie was already in the

bathroom. She added a little makeup and lip gloss. Then she went into the front room to wait for Carson.

"Where are you going?" her mom said, looking up from her mystery novel that she was reading in the living room.

"A picnic," Evie said. "I don't know where yet."

Her mom nodded. "You seem very . . . eager."

Evie shrugged.

Her mom put a bookmark in the novel, and closed her book. "Isn't Carson moving here soon?"

"Yes . . ."

Her mom lifted an eyebrow.

"Don't look at me like that," Evie said. "And don't say what you're going to say."

"All right." Her mom smiled, though. "I think it's great. I mean, Carson Hunt will be an excellent neighbor."

Evie groaned. She didn't want to think about the future right now. She wanted to think about what Carson had said about taking things a day at a time. But when she heard the rumble of his truck approaching, her pulse skittered all over the place, and she was out the door before he could pull to a stop.

She had to force herself to walk slowly, casually, down the steps. Her eyes were glued to the man who climbed out of the driver's seat and walked around the truck to open the passenger door for her. He wore a white T-shirt and faded jeans. And, yep, cowboy boots and his hat.

Okay, so he was beautiful, but that didn't mean she needed to ogle him. He might get too big of a head.

"Ready?" he said as she neared, his gaze perusing the length of her.

"Yep." She smiled, and he smiled back. Which melted her heart, if there was anything left to melt.

She moved past him and climbed into the truck, but not

before he'd put his hand at the small of her back. She wanted to pause and breathe him in, but she was pretty sure her mom could see them through the living room window. And who knew where her dad and brothers were.

She settled onto the seat, and while Carson walked around to the driver's side, she clipped on her seatbelt.

He climbed in and glanced over at her before shifting into drive.

"Hungry?" he asked.

"Yes," she said. "Did you give up on the picnic?"

"Nope," he said. "There's a basket in the bed of the truck."

She turned to see that, sure enough, a wicker basket was in the back. "Wow, I'm impressed."

"Just wait until you see what's inside." He waggled his eyebrows.

She laughed, then she reached for his hand—a bold move on her part. And her heart flipped as he easily linked their fingers.

When they reached the end of the lane, he said, "Where to, sweetness?"

"Left." She suddenly knew where she wanted to take him. In high school, she used to walk through the park and to the river that ran past all of Prosper. There was a section where she could always find alone time. Once she got back home, family and chores and homework would take up every moment of her thinking time.

It wasn't long before they reached the end of the road. "We'll have to walk a little way," she said as Carson pulled to a stop.

"No problem."

She climbed out of the truck before he could come around and open her door.

When he lifted the picnic basket out of the bed of the truck, she said, "Can I peek inside?"

"No way," he said, keeping the basket closed as he grabbed a blanket from the back of the truck as well. Then with his other hand, he grasped hers. "Where are we going?"

"Just a place I used to come to a lot—you know, when I didn't want to be found."

Carson glanced down at her. "You're showing me your secret hideout?"

"Yep."

His smile was slow as he drew her close. "Why?"

She leaned even closer, her clothing brushing against his. "Holt told me about your conversation, and I figured that a man who could put my brother in his place is a man who gets the real tour of Prosper."

Carson's smile widened. "Well, then I'm honored, ma'am."

She raised up on her toes and brushed her lips against his. They didn't embrace or hold each other—just a soft, tame kiss between them. But it was perfect.

Then, Evie snatched his hat and plunked it on top of her own head.

Carson grabbed for the hat, but she leapt away, laughing.

"Fine," he said. "You look better in it anyway."

Evie smirked and continued walking. She led him through a few trees, and soon, they'd arrived at the river, where she approached the bank and watched the meandering water. Memories flashed through her mind as she remembered some of the times she'd come here. Times of distress, anger, and even times of happiness, like when she'd found out she'd gotten into college on an academic scholarship. Or the time after prom when she'd been so mad at her brothers. And the time she came to sit and think for a couple of hours after finding out about her mom's cancer.

The memories were all there, shifting and moving like the flow of the river.

And now, she'd make a new memory. She looked over her shoulder to see Carson spreading a blanket on the ground, then setting the picnic basket in the middle. She still couldn't believe he'd suggested a picnic. It was so . . . quaint and sweet.

His gaze met hers, and she felt her cheeks heat up, but she didn't shift her gaze as he approached. Carson slipped an arm around her from behind, then he lifted the hat from her head.

She laughed, and he tossed it toward the blanket.

"I think we've got plenty of shade here."

And they did. The temperature was perfect, neither cold nor hot, and the river only added to the ambiance of the clear blue sky above.

Carson's other hand slid around her waist, and he drew her against him. She leaned back and closed her eyes, relishing in the feel of his warm chest and arms around her. New memories—this was good.

"This place is beautiful," Carson said, resting his chin on her shoulder so that his voice rumbled next to her ear.

A warm shiver sent goose bumps across her skin. "Yeah, I think it's my favorite place in Prosper."

His hold tightened, and she rested her arms on top of his. They didn't speak for a moment, only the sound of the river between them.

"Thanks for talking to my brother," she said.

"You're welcome," Carson said, a smile in his tone. "I wasn't sure how that little conversation was going to go. Whether I might have to take the topic to your dad."

"Would you have done that?"

"Absolutely."

Evie turned in his arms, and rested her hands on his shoulders. "You know, I should be fighting my own battles."

"Oh, you already are," Carson said, his dark eyes fastened on hers. "But I'm also going to defend what's mine."

She quirked a brow. "You did not just say that, Carson Hunt."

"What if I did?" he asked in a low, teasing tone.

"Then I'd say you're worse than my brothers."

He slid one hand up her back, then stopped at the nape of her neck. "Your brothers have good hearts and good intentions," he said. "But like I told Holt, your decisions have to be yours, and yours alone. No matter what."

"So, you don't care where I accept a job or decide to live?"

"Oh, I care very much." Carson winked.

"Hmmm. Good to know." She loved the amusement in his dark eyes, but she saw something more there, something deeper, more permanent. "Are you going to try to convince me to move back home?"

"Will it make a difference?" he asked, his mouth curving.

Evie released a small sigh. "One day at a time, right?"

"Right."

"Does this mean you've told your grandpa you're working for him?"

"All I've told him so far was that this spring break is for me to gather information and consider my options." Carson's hand threaded through her hair, and the sensation of his touch fluttered across her skin. "Nothing has been decided or promised."

Evie ran her fingers along his smooth jaw. "You shaved."

"I did."

She kissed him then, because it was impossible not to. Carson's mouth was warm and welcoming as he kissed her back. The sound of the river, the stillness of the air all created a brand new memory. One that she'd cherish always. She never thought the man who kissed her first would be the man she wanted a relationship with. Boyfriend, girlfriend . . . that sounded too serious, too permanent. It meant that things would be more complicated and feelings would be involved. And hearts.

As it was, her heart was skipping every other beat right now.

Carson's other hand anchored at her hip, and she pressed into him, wanting this moment, this memory, to last forever. She loved being in his arms, loved the way he made her feel, but was she wearing rose-colored glasses? Becca told her to not stress over it, to just enjoy being with a hot man who was also sweet.

Which, of course, Carson was. But he hadn't backed down from Holt. And it was pretty obvious that Carson liked *her.* If the way his kissing made her feel like the only woman in the world was any indication.

She had no one else to compare him to, but she didn't need to. Carson Hunt was the real deal. But he was most likely moving to Prosper to work for and take care of his grandad. And . . . she had to tell him about the email from the San Antonio newspaper. Because if he knew, then he might not be taking her on picnics and arguing her case against her brothers.

Her rumbling stomach caught Carson's attention.

"Okay, okay, we'll get you fed." He chuckled as he drew away.

She grabbed his hand, though, and he squeezed. She was already missing being in his arms, which was ridiculous. This crush was doing crazy things to her mind and emotions.

Carson knelt over the picnic basket and began to unload it. Two water bottles, a couple of sandwiches, which Evie discovered were turkey and lettuce, and a few red apples.

"Sorry it's not more fancy, but you didn't give me much notice."

"Whatever," Evie said with a laugh. "You're the one who suggested a picnic. Plus, this is perfect."

"Nothing's better than turkey on white." Carson unwrapped his sandwich and took a huge bite.

Evie grinned. She unwrapped her own sandwich and took a bite. "Pretty good."

"And a pretty good view, too."

But Carson wasn't looking at the blue-green river or the wildflowers lining the riverbank. He was gazing at her.

18

CARSON DIDN'T WANT TO go back to reality, or head home to start working with Grandad, or face the fact that spring break was almost over. But they'd been at the river for at least an hour, and the longer he stayed secluded with Evie, the more his mind turned over possibility after possibility.

Maybe Evie would work somewhere else for a year, then realize she wanted to return to Prosper. And him, of course. Or maybe when she met with the principal at the Prosper middle school, she'd have a change of heart.

Or maybe she'd fall madly in love with Carson and not care about where she lived anymore.

He could only dream.

Evie was currently sitting on a rock near the river, her feet in the water, while he packed up the picnic basket, then folded the blanket. Her blonde hair stirred in the breeze, and he only wanted to sit by her and bury his face in the soft strands. He wanted to kiss her for the rest of the day, and convince her to stay in Prosper.

But right now, he could tell she had something on her mind. She'd been flirty and affectionate the first part of their picnic, but then she'd gone to the river and sat, watching the water flowing.

There was nothing else he could do to stall and give her more time, so he sat next to her on the rock. Not saying anything and not touching her.

But she leaned against him, resting her head against his shoulder, and looping her arm through his. So he rested his hand on her knee, trying to ignore how nervous he suddenly felt.

"Are you okay?" he asked.

"Not really."

His heart froze. "What's wrong, Evie?"

She released a slow breath. "I got an interview with the *San Antonio Daily News.*"

His heart resumed a slow beat. "That's good, right? Aren't they at the top of your list?"

"They are," she said in a quiet voice, "so I should be elated, right?"

"And you aren't."

"I'm not." She lifted her head and met his gaze. "I thought I'd be jumping from excitement, but I'm dreading the interview. They'll see right through me. I have no experience, and they're going to be expecting great things from day one."

Carson knew he shouldn't smile at her worries—they were irrational because she'd be excellent—so he kept his gaze sober as he listened. When the breeze stirred her hair about her face, he brushed some of it from her cheek. "Do the interview," he said, although it was the last thing he wanted to encourage because he'd love her to move to Prosper, "and see what you think."

"Yeah . . ." She gave him a small smile, but her eyes started to water.

"You'll be amazing," he said. "And they'll be lucky if they get you."

She only bit her lip.

"Evie," he whispered, leaning close and touching their foreheads. "You worry too much. Everyone gets these kinds of jitters and doubts. You've spent four years getting ready."

"Are you just saying that to make me feel better?" she whispered.

He smiled, then tilted his head to kiss her cheek. "Yes, but it's also completely true. Do a couple of sample graphics and take them to the meeting. They'll know right away if you're a good fit."

She moved her hand slowly up his arm, then rested her hand on his bicep. She blinked a few times, and Carson was glad to see that new tears hadn't appeared. "Why did I meet you at the absolutely worst time ever?"

Carson raised his brows. "You mean at the football party?"

She smirked. "No. Right before I graduate."

"Maybe . . . it's the opposite," he said. "Maybe we met at the perfect time."

She bit her lip as she gazed at him, then said, "I should get back. I need to help my mom with dinner. Are you guys coming?"

"Are we invited?"

Her smile was coy. "I'm inviting you."

"Then the answer is yes," Carson said in a lighthearted tone. But he didn't feel lighthearted. Soon, they'd be going back to school and getting even closer to the inevitable.

He gathered up the basket and blanket while Evie put her shoes back on. Together, they walked back to the truck.

"It's after three," she said, checking her phone.

"Yeah?"

"Do you mind stopping by the school on the way back? I'm going to pop in and say hi to the principal. I promised my mom I would, and I don't want it to be a formal interview situation."

"All right." Carson eyed her, wondering what she was thinking. He was glad she was stopping in, but it seemed more of a formality than anything. "Do you want me to come with you?"

"It will literally take five minutes," she said. "If the principal is even there. School got out about fifteen minutes ago."

The drive to the school was quiet, and Carson wondered what she was thinking about. But he didn't feel like he could intrude right now.

"Thanks," she said as he pulled in front of the school and stopped.

She slipped out of the truck, and he watched her hurry toward the school. He hoped . . . he didn't know what he hoped. That she changed her mind about Prosper? That she'd stick up for her goals? That she'd be happy whatever she chose? Yeah, that was what he hoped.

Despite his growing fondness of her, and apparent attachment if his constant focus on her was an indicator, he wanted what was best for her.

It wasn't five minutes that he waited, but twenty. He could have maybe read some articles for one of his homework projects, but instead, he watched the comings and goings of the small town. The place was downright quiet, and peaceful.

When Evie finally emerged from the school, she was walking with another woman. The two approached the truck, and Carson didn't know if he was supposed to roll down the window, or get out. So he climbed out and walked around to the sidewalk.

The woman with Evie was petite with short, dark hair.

Her red-framed glasses matched the red blouse she wore with no-nonsense black pants.

"Carson, this is Bev Jarvis," Evie said. "She's the principal here."

"Great to meet you," he said, stepping forward and shaking her hand.

"Nice to meet you, too," Ms. Jarvis said in a mellow tone. "I've heard of your grandfather. The town appreciates his investment in the arena."

"I'll pass the news along to him," Carson said, glancing at Evie and trying to gauge how the conversation between the two of them had gone.

They said goodbye to Ms. Jarvis, and Carson opened the truck door for Evie. She slipped past him without a word on how things had gone.

When he climbed into the truck, she glanced over at him.

"What?" he asked. "How did it go?"

"She was really nice and said she has the funds to bring on a part-time graphic designer, but there are other roles in the school I could fill, so I'd have a full-time salary," Evie said, her voice sounding too happy, too cheerful. "I told her I wasn't ready to move to Prosper yet, but she wants to keep in touch anyway."

Carson's heart sank at the part about not moving to Prosper, but he liked that the door had been left open. "That sounds perfect," he said, his own smile becoming more false by the moment. "It will be nice to have that door open if you ever need it."

"Exactly." Evie leaned her head back and folded her arms. "My mom will be glad I stopped in, and now I can tell her I did."

Carson nodded. "What did you think about the school?"

"Oh, not much has changed," Evie continued in her

bright tone. "Still the same old floors and lockers. Lots of memories there."

Carson pulled onto Main Street, then glanced at her. "Was that hard?"

"Hard?" She gave a flippant shrug. "No. It was strange, though; I think I can say that."

"Evie—"

"I should get back," she said. "My mom probably thinks I've abandoned her, and I should help with dinner preparations. Maybe after, we can go to Racoons."

"To the battle of the bands that aren't really bands?" Carson wanted to figure out what was bothering Evie, but now she was talking about Racoons, a place she said she didn't want to go to.

Evie smiled too brightly. "I'll introduce you around, so when you come back here, you'll already know a bunch of people."

"Okay," he said, his heart twisting for some reason. What had happened in that school to have her acting like this?

Evie popped open her door the second he stopped at her ranch. "Thanks for the picnic, and plan on Racoons after dinner. It'll be fun."

"Evie, wait—"

But she'd opened the door and hopped down. She waved, then shut the door and hurried to the front porch. Carson watched her disappear inside. He wasn't even sure what had just happened.

He tossed his hat onto the bench and scrubbed a hand through his hair. Then he drove back to his grandad's place, only to find him on the phone with what sounded like a building contractor.

Carson went into his bedroom and dug out his laptop from the backpack he'd brought. He logged on, then connected to the hotspot on his phone. Moments later, he'd looked up the *San Antonio Daily News*, where Evie was interviewing next week. He scrolled through the website, and clicked on several featured links. The graphics had an outdated feel, and surely, Evie would bring a fresh look to them. From all that he could see, Evie would probably enjoy working there.

And he would miss her.

He knew that now. The connection he had with her in a short time already felt deeper than what he'd had with Stacee. Maybe it was because he was older, or had been through some harder things.

Carson sighed as he considered his options. There were really only two. Move to Prosper to work and be with his grandad. Or . . . not move to Prosper so he could be closer to Evie. But would she even want him around? That last few minutes in the truck had felt like she'd made up her mind about something, but wasn't sharing it yet.

Carson shut down the laptop and headed out of his bedroom. His grandad was still on the phone, sitting on a barstool with paperwork spread before him. Carson set about doing the dishes in the sink. The place didn't have a dishwasher, so he did them by hand.

When his grandad was finally off the phone, Carson said, "How are the plans going?"

"Good," Grandad said. "I should have all the bids by next week, then I can decide who to work with. They're promising the job completion in two months, but you'll be here by then and can help oversee it."

Carson nodded. "Right. We need to talk about that."

"Oh? Sounds serious." Grandad shifted on the barstool and clasped his hands atop the counter.

"I want to know what my options are with working for you," Carson said.

"Is this about Evie?"

Grandad didn't miss much.

Carson braced his hands on the counter across from Grandad. "Yeah."

Grandad nodded and rubbed at his chin. The white whiskers there had never been shaven clean that Carson could remember. "When I met your grandmother, nothing could have changed my mind about her."

Carson had heard plenty about his grandmother, a woman he'd never met. From all descriptions, she was a no-nonsense woman. She was the love of Grandad's life, and when she was gone, he never remarried. Never wanted to.

"I wish I could have met her," Carson said.

"She would have told you to follow your heart, son," Grandad said. "I want you here, with me, in Prosper. But if a man has found his person, his woman, that's more important."

Carson exhaled and held his grandad's steady gaze. "You've done so much for me and Rhett. You dropped everything when we needed you, and you've taken care of us ever since."

Grandad rose to his feet and walked around the counter, then he placed a hand on Carson's shoulder. "And I'd do it again in a heartbeat. The beauty of being self-employed is that I can make choices. I'm not tied to one place, one house, or one office. Prosper is where I want to retire, since I'm getting on in years. And yes, I'd love to have my only grandson at my beck and call. But I don't mean my decision to be a decision for you as well. Go out and live your life, son."

Carson blew out a breath, then placed a hand atop his grandad's. "Thanks for your blessing. I still don't know what my final decision will be."

"Don't make a final decision, then," he said. "One day at a time. It's the Hunt way."

"I thought it sounded familiar," Carson said with a smile. "That's what I told Evie, too, but I think she sees the only way forward is to not create more ties to Prosper."

Grandad gave a curt nod, then a cheeky grin. "You've got your work cut out for you, son. But no woman is worth it who doesn't take a bit of work."

"I've no doubt," Carson said.

"I'm just glad you've moved on from Stacee," Grandad said. "And that you've healed enough to believe in happiness again."

"I've always believed in it," Carson said.

"Perhaps. But you've never allowed yourself to trust in it."

Carson folded his arms with a sigh. "It's a risk, especially with Evie."

"Yes," Grandad said. "But you go out there and show her that you're the man for her."

"Easier said than done."

Grandad shrugged and picked up the pack of cigarettes that he'd left on the kitchen table. After removing one, he said, "If it's right, then things will fall into place."

Carson knew his grandad was right, but the wait was painful.

19

EVIE IGNORED BECCA'S PHONE call. Yeah, she should answer it, but her mind was a whirl. Going into that school had opened a flood of memories, ones that she hadn't cared to recall. She still felt out of sorts just thinking about it.

When her phone rang a second time, Evie eyed it. What did Becca want? Finally, she snatched up the phone from her bed and answered it.

"Hi, what's up?" she asked.

"Oh, I was going to leave a voicemail," Becca said. "Guess what?"

"What?" Evie said, hiding a sigh as she leaned against the stack of pillows on her bed.

"I got my acceptance to medical school!"

"What?" Evie sat up fully. "That's amazing! Congratulations!"

"I can't believe it," Becca gushed. "I mean, I sort of can, but I think I'm in shock."

"This is so great," Evie said. "When do you start and all that?"

"August, but I have to sign up for lab work right away,"

Becca said. "Everyone says that there's a waiting list for the morning labs, so unless I want to be there late at night . . ."

Evie listened as Becca continued to tell her the details of what her first year of medical school would be like, and she felt pride expanding in her chest. She hadn't doubted Becca, but now that it was actually happening, it was amazing.

Becca had a plan, a direction, and a future career, and Evie wondered how that would affect their friendship. They'd both be moving on and no longer roommates. The thought was sobering.

All that was familiar to Evie would change before she knew it.

"So what's new with Carson?" Becca asked.

Evie blinked. She hadn't caught the past few things that Becca had said. What had been the segue to talking about Carson?

"He's great," Evie said. "We went on a picnic today." She glossed over the details, even though Becca seemed thoroughly impressed about the picnic. "And I'm actually heading back to campus tomorrow."

"What? You have another whole weekend."

"Yeah, I know," Evie said. "But it's too hard to get any homework done here, and I'm feeling the pressure from my mom to accept a job at the local school." After coming home, she had told her mom about meeting with Ms. Jarvis, and her mom had lit up and asked a million hopeful questions.

"Oh, Evie," Becca said, her tone sounding like a sigh.

"What?"

"You're doing it again."

Evie's neck prickled. She knew what Becca was talking about.

"You like a guy, and just when he's interested in you, you run."

"No," Evie said immediately. "I'm not running. We've kissed . . . a lot. And things are good between us."

"Did he ask you to reconsider your decision about Prosper?"

"Nothing of the sort," Evie said. "In fact, it's much worse than that."

"What do you mean?" Becca asked in a concerned tone.

"He's happy that I got the interview with the *San Antonio Daily News*," Evie said. "In fact, he said they'd be lucky to have me."

Becca didn't respond for a moment, then she said, "Does he know you're going back tomorrow?"

"No one does," Evie said, feeling defensive again. "I'll tell my family after dinner. No reason to be the focus of the dinner conversation."

"Well . . . this is your decision, obviously, but I hope you at least give Carson a chance."

Evie closed her eyes, grateful that Becca couldn't see her in person. "I'm not running. I'm just cutting spring break a couple of days short."

Becca's non-reply was a reply by itself, and by the time Evie had hung up with her friend, she was feeling hollowed out.

But this was what it was like to make a decision that someone didn't agree with. It would be much easier to cave to everyone's expectations and wishes, as she had her entire life, to avoid the self-doubt. She could do this; she *would* do this.

After dinner, of course.

The dinner hour crawled by, and Evie hated every minute of it. Not even Ruby was enough of a distraction, since she was seated on the other end of the table. Instead, Carson sat by her, and although his arm was half-draped over her chair part of the time, he otherwise didn't touch her. He mostly talked to

Holt and Lane, though there were plenty of times they included her in the conversation.

Evie kept her answers short, all the while wanting to get away, to have time to herself. Maybe she could even go back tonight. But she knew there was no late-night bus service, and she hadn't even broached the topic with either of her brothers to give her a ride.

Carson would probably offer when he found out, but then he might cut his spring break short, too, and that would completely defeat the purpose . . . The purpose of returning to campus alone without her roommate Becca, and without the man next to her who'd wrapped his way around every part of her life, making her second-guess what she'd decided a long time ago.

"You're going to Racoons?" Lane asked, laughter in his tone. "Does Evie know?"

Carson glanced at her. "She's the one who suggested it."

"I did," Evie said, putting her fork down. She'd hardly eaten, anyway. "Y'all should come."

Lane's brows furrowed. "I am going; I just didn't think *you* would go."

"Why not?" Evie said in a flippant tone. Lane was moving the irritation meter higher than she had patience for.

Lane shrugged and picked up his glass of water. "Thought you were keeping Carson all to yourself."

Evie's face burned, not just because of what her brother said, but because it was at the dinner table in front of the whole family. She laughed a fake laugh and asked for her dad to pass the salt. After salting her already-salted chicken, the conversation had moved on. Yet, she felt Carson's questioning glances.

She just had to get through tonight, and tomorrow, then she'd be free of all the memories that going into the school had brought back like a blow. Even now, she felt shaky at the thought of walking those halls again. What had she been thinking? Marching in to talk to Ms. Jarvis like it was something she'd done every day.

As the family conversations swirled about her, her mind replayed the first day that she'd shown up to school wearing makeup, with a perm in her hair. Evie had been a week past her thirteenth birthday, and her mom had finally given her permission to wear makeup. But at school, she got the opposite reaction that she'd hoped for. No one stopped and told her she looked pretty. The guys didn't suddenly notice her. In fact, the popular girls had smirked and talked about her behind her back. Including Jana. Who was apparently still friends with Barb and would be at Racoons tonight.

Evie might as well get it all over with. Face her past, then hightail it out of town in the morning. She admitted she was curious about Jana, but mostly, Evie wanted to prove to herself that she could go to a major social event and not be the shy girl in the corner.

She was weeks away from an undergraduate degree, and she was potentially working for the top newspaper in San Antonio.

"All right, then," Holt said. "Everyone have a good night. We've got to get this little girl to bed."

"I'm not a little girl," Ruby declared from her booster chair. "I'm your little darlin'."

Holt chuckled, and he moved to help Macie clean up her daughter's mess.

Evie watched the easy way that Holt and Macie acted around Ruby. For a moment, her heart strings tugged for Knox, but he'd effectively cut himself off from his own daughter. So it was Holt who Ruby was growing closer to every day.

"I'll see you tomorrow?" Macie said, walking around the table and touching Evie's shoulder.

Evie loved that about Macie. No matter what was going on in their big family, Macie always singled her out.

"Yep," Evie said, and inside, she thought, *if you're here really early in the morning.* She didn't want to make any announcements just yet. She'd tell Carson after Racoons, then she'd figure out her ride later on.

When Mr. Hunt was preparing to leave, he said he'd walk if Carson wanted to stick around longer.

"Oh, I've got to get ready," Evie said. "So you two go on ahead."

Finally, she was alone again in her bedroom. She sat on the edge of her bed and opened her emails on her phone.

She reread the one from *San Antonio Daily News* once again, waiting for that elation to kick in, but all she felt was nerves. Maybe Carson was right, and she needed to believe in herself more.

Evie released a slow breath.

Carson wasn't her first crush, but he was her first kiss, so maybe that was why she was feeling so attached to him. But deep down, she knew she was making excuses. Ones that she was believing in right now. Finally, she moved to her closet, where she'd stashed the few belongings that she'd brought. She pulled on jeans that were still clean, then buttoned up a violet shirt. Next, she headed to the bathroom and added a few more waves to her hair with a curling wand.

She was as ready now as she was ever going to be. She didn't know who she'd be running into tonight, but she planned to not let any of it bother her. As a visitor, after all, she was no longer emotionally invested in any of these people. Aside from her family, she didn't care. Shouldn't care.

She sent Carson a text. *Do you want to meet there or go together?*

I'll pick you up in ten if that's okay.

Ok.

Exhaling, she slipped her phone into her pocket and headed down the hallway to the front room to find her parents both there. They were sitting on the couch as if waiting to talk to her.

She slowed her step and turned to them. "I shouldn't be too late."

"Have a seat, dear," her mom said. "Holt brought something to our attention."

Evie's stomach plummeted. She'd wanted to move on from all of this and not rehash it again. But she sat down, facing her parents.

"Is what he said true?" her dad said, leaning forward. His rugged face was creased with concern. "About how you've been feeling like we don't trust you with decisions?"

"Yeah," she said. "It wasn't really with you guys as much, just with my brothers growing up. And I guess a little bit now, too."

"I don't mean to pressure you into moving back to Prosper," her mom said. "But we'd love to have you here, of course. We do trust your decisions, though, and we definitely know you'll do great things wherever you land."

"Thanks," Evie said, swallowing against the growing lump in her throat. "I appreciate that."

"Sweet pea," her dad said, rising to his feet and crossing over. "You've got our full support, whatever you decide to do."

She stood and stepped into his arms and hugged him. Relief swept through her. Her dad pulled her close and patted her back. "And that Carson Hunt. He's a fine fellow."

Evie smiled. "Yeah, he is."

Next, her mom hugged her.

When she stepped away from her parents, she said, "I'm going back to campus tomorrow morning."

Her mom immediately began to protest, but her dad said, "Heidi, let her finish."

"I need a couple of days to myself to catch up on homework and get ready for an interview on Monday." She told them about the interview, and soon, both of her parents were smiling.

Had it really been this simple all along—that she could open up a little, and her resentment would wash away?

No, she knew it wasn't that simple. She still had Racoons to face, and who knew what she'd encounter there. Just then, she heard a truck rumbling up the drive. She glanced over to see that sure enough, Carson had arrived.

Her heart immediately soared, then plummeted. Carson had put the wrench in all of her plans, and tonight might very well be the last night they spent together. If the interview went great on Monday, then really, it would be selfish to keep dating Carson. Wouldn't she be leading him on?

One day at a time, she whispered to herself as she headed outside. But was that fair to either of them?

Carson was already out of his truck, and Evie drew in a breath at the sight of him. His navy button-down made no secret of the breadth of his shoulders, and his dark jeans only made him look taller. He wore a nicer cowboy hat than she'd ever seen him wearing.

"You're all dressed up," she teased.

His gaze met hers, and heat flashed through her, because she could see he was appreciating her as much as she was appreciating him. He also smelled amazing.

"You look beautiful," Carson said, reaching for her hand and wrapping his warm fingers around hers.

Evie's heart jolted. She shouldn't be reacting like this to him. Tonight was about introducing him to more people in Prosper so that when *he* returned, not *her*, he'd have a wider base of those he'd met.

But the warm tingles spread throughout her, regardless. And if she didn't suspect her parents could see her from the living room window, she might steal a kiss. She walked to the passenger side with him as the sun's setting rays disappeared beyond the horizon, leaving a soft purple twilight.

Once inside the truck, Evie rattled off the people who would probably be there. None of them had been her true friends, but she'd know everyone's names. Carson was quiet for the most part, and when he stopped the truck across from Racoons, the place was already hopping.

Music boomed from the open door, and the side of the road Racoons was on was filled with parked cars. Lights spilled from the square windows, and a group of people was outside, smoking together.

Evie didn't recognize them off hand, but they were still across the street and the sky was nearly dark. The stars were beginning to appear, filling the sky like a glittering carpet.

Maybe they could just skip the whole battle of the bands scene and walk along the river, hand in hand. Of course, that sort of solitude with Carson would only make it harder to leave in the morning.

"Ready?" she said in a bright voice, releasing his hand and reaching for the door handle.

"Hang on, Evie."

She looked over at him, and the depths of his eyes were nearly black.

"We don't have to go if you don't want to," he said in a low voice.

"I'm fine," she said. "Plus, I can introduce you to people our age."

He held her gaze for a second, like he wanted to say something else, but instead, he nodded. "All right. Know anytime, we can leave."

"Okay." Evie didn't want to dwell on how sweet Carson was being. Well, he was always sweet.

"Wait for me," he said, opening his door.

So she did, as her pulse began to thud. She was about to go into Racoons. Would it be easier with Carson at her side? Yeah, it would create a lot more questions, but at least she wouldn't be fending for herself, or having to deal with the pickup scene.

Her door opened, and Carson was standing there. She put her hand in his and slid down next to him. He didn't move back or give her space.

"Did I tell you that you look beautiful?"

She lifted her chin to meet his gaze. He hadn't shaved that evening, so his dark stubble had started to show through. Her hand had a mind of its own, and she ran her fingers across his jaw.

He leaned down, slowly, as if waiting for her permission, then kissed the edge of her mouth.

Evie placed her hand on his chest. "Easy, cowboy."

"Come on, let's ditch this place, sweetness."

"Not tonight." Evie pushed past him, then grasped his hand and tugged him with her. Tonight might be her last date with Carson, but everyone would know they were together.

20

CARSON COULDN'T READ EVIE. Not that he thought he'd ever know the inner workings of a woman's mind, but she was either hot or cold. He wished she would open up to him. Ever since they'd stopped by the school, something was off, but she seemed so focused on this night at Racoons. So he'd go with her, meet whoever she introduced him to, then hopefully, when they were alone again, she'd clue him into why she was so jittery.

It had been a while since Carson had been to a bar. Definitely nothing since breaking up with Stacee. As he approached the bar with its thumping music, his pulse dialed up a notch. Rhett would have loved this place, Carson could already tell. His brother might have even entered the battle of the bands with his guitar—a guitar that was stowed somewhere.

The inside of the bar was large, with a balcony overlooking a dance floor, and tables lining the exterior of the room. It smelled like every other bar, with cloying perfumes and cologne, mixed with beer. A platform was at the far side—and Carson assumed it was the makeshift stage. No one was playing right now, although a couple of cowboys were gathered on the platform, seeming to be tuning their guitars.

The music that thumped came through the speakers, and the colored lights shifted across the dance floor. The place was surprisingly crowded and filled with people in their twenties and thirties.

A group of older cowboys sat in one corner, hunched over their drinks. They looked like they were about to bail due to the influx of younger people.

"Is it always this busy?" Carson said, close to Evie's ear. "Where are all these people from?"

"Surrounding towns," she said.

He felt her stiffen beside him, and that's when he saw the woman they'd met at the diner—Barb or Barbie—approaching, with two other women with her. They all wore what looked like cocktail dresses, which felt way too overdressed for a small-town bar.

Ironically, Barb's face was made up like a Barbie doll, and her glittering blue dress shined in the spotlights.

"You made it, Evie!" Barb practically sang out. Then she air-kissed Evie.

Next, Barb turned to Carson, slipped an arm about his waist, and squeezed him in a side hug.

Um . . .

"Hi, there," he said.

"Oh, don't *hi there* me, pumpkin," Barb cooed. "We're pretty much neighbors." She motioned to the two women who'd come with her. "This is Patsy and Jana."

Patsy's dark hair was short and stuck out every which way—a fashion statement, Carson guessed. Jana was a voluptuous redhead who looked as if she'd experimented with her mom's makeup. What was up with the women in this town and their layers of makeup?

"Oh, wow, I'm so excited to meet you," Jana said, stepping forward to squeeze Carson's arm.

Patsy giggled, then took a swig of her drink, practically teetering on her heels.

"Don't mind Patsy," Barb said. "She's already on her third drink."

Patsy giggled again, as if to support that statement.

Now, Carson remembered with full clarity why he hadn't been to a bar in a long, long time.

"Right." Jana peered up at him, standing surprisingly close, as if the conversation was just between them. "Patsy enjoys her fun, and Barb is the perfect host. Me, though, I'm just the girl next door."

"Hi, Jana," Evie said, her tone cutting across all the weird flirty stuff going on.

Jana dropped her hand from Carson's bicep and slowly turned to look at Evie. "Oh. My. Gosh. Evie Prosper? Wow. You've, um, grown up."

Evie's smile was tight. "So have you."

Carson looked between the women. He guessed Jana to be the same age as Evie. Had they gone to school together? Been friends? There didn't seem to be any love lost between the two women. Besides, Evie's hand had tightened in his.

"It was nice to meet you all, but if you'll excuse us, ladies, we have some dancing to do." He felt Evie's surprise, but this wasn't the moment to explain.

He drew her along with him toward the dance floor.

"You really want to dance?" she asked when they were out of earshot of the three women.

"Of course, this is my favorite song."

Evie's smile was faint, but it was there, and that was good enough for Carson. The music had slowed down, which was perfect, and Carson drew her close. Tucking her under his chin, he kept one hand on the small of her back and the other clasping hers against his chest.

As they moved to the music, Carson's body warmed at the feel of Evie's curves against him. She was beautiful on the outside, but he loved everything about her, even when she was holding back some sort of emotion from him. It only made him more protective of her. And he would wait until she was ready to tell him, trusted him enough to confide.

"Thank you," Evie whispered against his neck.

"For what?"

"For . . . taking me away from them," she said. "Those girls were the popular group in school."

"Not your friends?"

"Heavens, no." Evie moved a tad closer.

Carson waited, but she didn't say anything else. Then the music shifted again, and seconds later, someone spoke into the mic on stage.

"Welcome to Racoons, folks," a heavyset man with an impressive mustache said. "We've got an exciting night for you."

Cheers and whistles went up from those around them, and Carson released Evie from his hold, keeping her hand in his, so they could turn and watch.

The man announced the first band, and two guys took their places. Both had guitars, and they began to plunk out a discordant tune. Carson tried not to wince, tried to stay open-minded. He was no music connoisseur, but how were the others enjoying this? Looking around, plenty of people were swaying or dancing to the music.

"You new around here?" a guy next to them asked. He was probably in his thirties, and his paisley shirt was purple and yellow—definitely a standout. His black cowboy hat had seen better days.

"I'm Carson Hunt," he said, holding out his hand.

The guy shook his hand. "Ah, you're ole man Hunt's grandson. I'm Briggs. Welcome to Prosper."

"Thanks," Carson said, but Briggs was no longer looking at him.

Briggs was staring at Evie with wide eyes. "Well, I'll be roped like a calf. If it isn't little Evie Prosper."

"Hi, Briggs," she said in a flat tone. "I saw you at Christmas, remember?"

"Oh, yeah, I do remember," Briggs said, looking her up and down with appreciation. "But you were hiding under a big sweater."

Carson frowned. Was this guy coming onto Evie?

She smirked. "You say the same thing to me every time you see me. Aren't you in the lineup tonight?"

"Sure am, sunshine." He grinned. "Y'all gonna vote for me?"

"If you're the best," Evie was quick to say.

Briggs chuckled. "Fair enough." He slapped Carson on the shoulder. "Well, you consider voting for me? Only if you think I'm the best." He winked and stepped away.

"What do you think?" a woman asked, sidling up to him.

Carson was surprised to see that Barb and Jana were back. No sign of Patsy.

"I'm hoping the talent gets better from here on out," Carson said.

Barb and Jana both laughed.

"Wait until you hear Briggs," Jana said, her smile wide and aimed in his direction.

"Is he good?"

Jana laughed, and Barb joined in. Apparently, everything Carson said was amusing.

"You might want to have a beer or two before he starts," Jana said, raising a hand to his arm. Again.

But Carson saw it coming and shifted. "Is that Lane?" he asked, spotting the Prosper brother coming into the bar.

Lane saw him at the same moment and headed in his direction. "You really did come, sis," he said to Evie.

"Lane Prosper," Jana said with a coy smile. It seemed her attention had shifted from Carson to Lane, which was fine with him. "You're looking fine."

"You are, too, Jana," Lane said with a generous smile. "Sorry, I've gotta steal Carson from you for a moment. Be right back, ladies."

Carson didn't have a chance to question where he was being taken before Lane steered him through the bar. He glanced back at Evie, but she seemed to be caught up in another conversation with Barb and Jana. He felt guilty about leaving her with two women she didn't seem to care for, but this was her town. Or used to be, anyway.

"Everyone, this is Carson Hunt," Lane declared when they paused in front of two tables that had been shoved together.

The cowboys at the table greeted him, and introductions continued, although Carson knew he probably wouldn't remember any of their names.

"Have a seat," Lane said, clapping him on the shoulder, and someone else shifted a chair toward him.

So Carson sat. Another guy scooted a beer toward him from the collection in the middle of the table.

"I'll go grab another round," Lane said, taking off toward the bar.

"You're Mr. Hunt's grandson?" one guy asked.

"That's me," Carson said, glancing over where Evie had been standing. The women had moved, and he scanned the room searching for her.

"How'd ya end up with Evie?" the guy continued.

Carson zeroed in on him. He guessed him to be late twenties. "What's your name again?"

The guy chuckled. "Douglas, but you can call me Deuce."

"Okay . . ."

"It's cause he's won the grand champion the past two years at the rodeo," one of the other guys piped up. "*After* Knox left town, of course."

Everyone at the table laughed.

Deuce merely nodded, a grin on his face.

"Are you gonna answer the question about Evie?" one of the others asked.

Carson glanced at Lane, but he was still at the bar, ordering more drinks.

"Well?" Deuce prompted.

Carson met the man's gaze. "We met at school, and I gave her a ride home."

"Looks like you did more than give her a ride home," Deuce said with a smirk.

Carson's neck burned hot. He'd never been in a bar fight, but this guy was pushing him to the edge. "I'll leave you to your drinks. Nice to meet y'all." He rose, but before he could step away from the table, Deuce spoke up again.

"Looks like you're a whipped pansy over the mayor's daughter," he drawled. "You think you can bribe the mayor into making changes in Prosper with your grandad's money?"

Carson spun around, and in an instant, he'd hauled Deuce to his feet by the collar. The guys at the table went silent, but he didn't care. It was taking all of his willpower to not plow his fist into the guy's cocky face.

"Don't talk about what you don't know," Carson said. "And always leave a woman out of it."

Someone whistled, but Carson was focused on Deuce.

The guy didn't even flinch. In fact, a slow smile lifted his mouth.

"Hey, now," Lane said, suddenly there, and putting himself between Carson and Deuce. "Douglas here is an old friend. Let's stay calm and work this out."

Carson still didn't release the guy, but he turned his gaze to Lane. "You need new friends." With that, he released Deuce and walked away.

He found Evie over by the bar, where the women had congregated. Her gaze was on him, and by the look in her eyes, he knew she'd seen him grab Deuce.

As he neared, Jana popped out of the group of women. "What happened between you and Deuce?"

"Nothing," he said, in a short tone. His gaze found Evie. "I should probably take off. You want to come or stay here with your friends?" He used the word *friends* lightly.

Evie hopped off the barstool in one second flat. "I'm coming." She grasped his hand and threw a half-smile to the other women. "See y'all later."

Carson was positive that Jana was pouting, and he didn't miss the snide glance she gave Evie as she passed by. What was that all about?

Barb only smiled. "Have fun, you two!"

Unfortunately, they had to pass by the guys' tables on their way out, but Carson kept his gaze forward as he walked through the crowd.

The cool evening air was welcome; so was leaving the less than pleasant music playing on the stage. They walked hand in hand to the truck, neither of them speaking. Carson was still trying to wrap his mind around what had just happened in Racoons. First, Barb and Jana, mostly Jana, were pretty awful to Evie. Then Deuce was downright rude, and Lane didn't even seem bothered by it one iota.

Carson opened the passenger door, and before Evie climbed in, she said, "Maybe Racoons wasn't such a good idea after all."

"Agreed," Carson said, everything in his body tense. He'd almost punched a man, and where would that have landed his reputation in Prosper? Yet, he'd happily do it if men like Deuce continued to say stupid stuff.

Evie put her hand on his chest. "Are you okay?" She looked genuinely concerned, and she'd dropped her falsely bright tone.

"I'm much better now."

Evie nodded and slipped past him, climbing into the truck. Then he shut the door. Before he took her back home, he had a few things to ask her.

21

EVIE WASN'T SURPRISED WHEN Carson suggested they talk. She'd seen the altercation between him and Douglas. She had no idea what it was about, but Carson was clearly still bothered by it.

He hadn't said much on the drive home, but before turning into the lane leading to her parents' house, he pulled off to the side of the road and turned off the truck's headlights.

"Who's Jana?" he asked.

Evie wasn't sure what she'd been expecting him to say first, but that wasn't it. "She's someone from school, like I told you."

"Why don't you like each other? What happened?"

Evie looked over at Carson. The only light inside the truck was the moonlight spilling in through the windows. He'd taken his hat off and scrubbed his hand through his hair, making him look adorably sexy.

Couldn't she just kiss him and forget all of this? Tomorrow, she'd be leaving and . . . she didn't want to remember her past.

Carson shifted so he was facing her, and his fingers played with her hair, his touch soft as he brushed a trail of warmth along her neck. "You told me you hated Prosper because it was such a small town, but I think there's more, Evie. Your brothers have been overprotective, yeah. But tonight, I saw something else. Something I didn't like."

"What?" she asked, her voice a near whisper.

"I saw a couple of women dismiss you as if you don't matter," he said. "And I heard a man disrespect you. Not one of those men at the table seemed bothered. Lane even claimed Deuce as a friend."

Her pulse was skittering all over the place. "What did Deuce say?"

"He implied that I was dating you to get to your dad," Carson said. "But the way he spoke about you was uncalled for. And the entire table of men let him do it, so I wonder what else you've gone through. You don't have to tell me anything, Evie. You can keep things as personal as you want, but next time some idiot mouths off about you, I'm not going to walk away. I don't care if it's a punk named Deuce or your own brother."

Evie was staring at him. "I don't think they meant any harm—"

Carson rested his hand on her shoulder. "Don't disparage yourself. Don't give them the benefit of the doubt. They're in the wrong, sweetness. Stop making excuses for them."

She lowered her gaze, the intensity in his eyes making her stomach tight and her throat hurt because she was close to tears. Carson was defending her because he was a good man. And those other guys . . . she hadn't even bothered to think about them, or worry about them, because she'd been with Carson.

At one point in high school, she thought that Douglas might like her. He'd never asked her out, or more clearly, never *tried* to ask her out. He was tight with Lane, and probably privy to whatever her brothers thought of guys with crushes on her. In fact, now that she was opening her memories, Douglas and Jana had gone to senior prom together. They'd seemed to be an item for a while, but Evie was too focused on graduating and leaving Prosper to follow their relationship arc.

"Jana and I were in the same grade," she said. "I was never one of the popular girls, but they started to pay more attention to me when my brothers got older. Especially Knox. He was the best in the town at rodeo, so everyone idolized him. Jana especially."

Carson didn't reply, just kept his hand on her shoulder as he listened.

"When she and Knox went out one night, the rumor was that he turned her down, for kissing, or maybe something else." Evie released a slow breath. "Somehow, it was my fault, and Jana started to find ways to make my life miserable. She'd load up my locker with stuff like bags of garbage. She also used to pretend to trip when I got near and bump into me. I'd be caught off-guard, so I'd drop my stuff."

"You were bullied?"

It wasn't really a question, more of a statement. Being bullied was such a buzz word now, but Evie guessed that was what had technically happened. "Yeah."

Carson closed his eyes and leaned his forehead against hers. "I'm sorry."

She shrugged, because what could she say really?

"Is that why you were so spooked when you came out of the school earlier today?"

Evie drew back. "How did you know?"

"You haven't been yourself since going in there," he said. "Did it trigger some memories?"

Evie leaned her head against the seat. "I didn't think I'd

be so affected. I went in and saw the row of lockers, and bam, it was like being hit by an avalanche. The memories flooded in, but it wasn't just the memories. It was that sickening feeling of helplessness I used to have. Like I couldn't do anything to change my circumstances. I had to keep reminding myself that there's nothing I can change about the past, and I'm a grown woman now."

"That doesn't mean the emotional part isn't still hard," Carson said. "These things take time to get through."

Evie nodded. She expected to feel numb after confessing to Carson, but instead, she felt lighter somehow. "Thanks for not thinking I'm a basket case."

Carson grasped her hand and brought it to his lips. "If anyone's a basket case, it's me."

She turned her head to meet his gaze. "Hardly."

"Tonight was the first night I stepped inside a bar, or any sort of social event, in two years," he said. "The only reason I went to that football party was to track down Devon."

Evie had no idea that he's stayed away from social stuff as well. She knew his brother had died and he'd broken up with his girlfriend soon after. He'd talked about hyper-focusing on football and school, which drove some of his friends away.

"So, what was it like, going into a place like Racoons?"

"Honestly?" he said in a quiet voice. "It made me realize that I've moved past the party scene and the single scene. I'm open to new friendships, sure, but not in that type of pickup scene. Everyone watching everyone else. Everyone assessing, judging, getting into each other's business."

"You mean small-town living?" She had a hard time keeping the bitterness out of her voice.

"If I ever live in Prosper, I'll not be hanging out at Racoons," Carson said. "At least, if the atmosphere stays the same."

Hold on. "What do you mean, *if* you live in Prosper. I thought you'd accepted your grandad's offer."

"I haven't officially committed," he said. "I'm keeping my options open."

This was news to Evie, and now her thoughts had scattered. If Carson wasn't in Prosper, then where would he be?

"Evie, I need to confess something."

She nearly stopped breathing. His tone was low, intimate, and his hand had settled on her hip. "Okay," she whispered.

"I don't want to be where you aren't," he said. "I know I said we'd take things one day at a time, and that's still the plan. But . . . I can't stop thinking about you. Even when I'm sleeping, I'm dreaming about you."

Evie's heart had risen to her throat. "Carson . . ." But she didn't know what to say, how to respond.

"I don't want to put pressure on you, and I told you I wouldn't," he said. "When you make your decision, it might influence mine." The edge of his mouth twitched. "But of course, you could always tell me no."

"No to what?"

"No to me following you around, asking you out, stealing kisses, just being with you." He trailed fingers over her collarbone in a whisper touch.

Her breathing had turned ragged. Carson had opened his heart to her, and she knew hers was already there, taking him in. But how was he okay with not moving to Prosper? She had seen how much his grandad meant to him. And now, Carson was waiting for her response. He'd put his feelings on the line.

She lifted a hand to his beautiful face, ran her fingers along the edge of his jaw, his whiskers soft yet rough beneath her touch. Her hand moved to his neck, then behind it, and the strands of his hair tickled her skin. He watched her, his eyes half-slitted, and he was still waiting. But what could she say? That she was foolishly smitten? That she had considered breaking every promise to herself, and moving back to Prosper, to be with him? This wasn't what he was asking.

"What do *you* want, truly?" she finally whispered. "Tomorrow? Next month? Next year?"

"You," he said, and there was no hesitation in his voice.

She kissed him, then. She couldn't give him the answer he was seeking, not yet, but she didn't think he was about to turn down her kissing. She was right. Carson immediately responded, covering her mouth with his. Drawing her in deep. His hand splayed across her hip as he pulled her closer, and she melted into him.

She looped both arms about his neck, memorizing the taste of him, the feel of him. Because she never wanted to forget *this*, no matter what her future brought. "Carson," she whispered when they both took a moment to breathe, and his hands were tangled in her hair and her face was pressed against his neck.

"Hmm?"

She loved the way his voice rumbled. "I'm going back to campus tomorrow. I have to sort things out in my mind before that interview. Away from my family and . . . everything."

Carson stilled, and she could practically hear him thinking, or perhaps arguing with himself.

Finally, he drew away enough that he could study her. "Do you want me to drive you? I can easily cut my trip short."

"No," she whispered. "Holt will take me. I texted him while we were at Racoons. He's coming at 7:00."

Carson gave a slight nod, but his jaw had tensed.

"Remember when you said we'd take things one day at a time?" she said.

"Yeah." His gaze searched hers, and she could see the wariness in his.

"That's what I'm doing," she said. "But I need to figure things out away from distractions and opinions and memories."

"Which am I?" he whispered.

"None of those, and all of those." Evie gave a half-laugh. "I don't know. I am a basket case, so you can't say I didn't warn you."

"You're an amazing and beautiful woman, Evie Prosper." Carson smoothed a hand over her hair, then his fingers lingered on her arm, his thumb caressing. "If Holt can't take you, I will. I can drop you off and come back here for the rest of the weekend, then see you Sunday night."

Right now wasn't the time for tears, so Evie blinked them back and said, "All right. If anything changes, I'll let you know."

Headlights flashed and bounced behind them, shining through the rear window. Carson released her and turned to peer out his window as a truck pulled up alongside them.

Lane had arrived.

Carson rolled down his window, and Lane did the same.

"What's going on?" Lane said. "Everything all right?"

"Fine," Carson said. "It's kind of you to check in on your sister."

Lane frowned. "I'm sorry about those guys. If I'd have known, I'd have . . ."

"You'd have *what*?" Carson shot back, his tone hard. "Thrown a punch? Bought them more beers? Sang kumbaya?"

"Hey, now," Lane said. "Deuce said he was sorry."

Evie felt the tension in Carson multiplying by the minute. "Carson . . ."

His eyes were still locked on her brother. "I didn't hear any apology, and if he did apologize, it was to the wrong person."

Lane exhaled. "You're right." He frowned. "Evie, I'm sorry about what my friends said about you and Carson."

"Thanks, Lane," Evie said. "I appreciate the apology."

Evie looked from her brother to Carson. The tension between the two had dissipated, but she could still sense the energy thrumming from Carson.

"And Carson's right," Lane continued. "I do need new friends. Not that I've seen them much since being in college, but things are going to change around here."

"Maybe," Evie said. "None of them have left Prosper, so it's like they're still in the high school void. Still petty and pitting themselves against each other."

"Yeah . . ." Lane said. "So I owe you guys lunch or dinner, or something. Does tomorrow work?"

Evie told him she was leaving, and Lane's brows pulled. "Is it because of me? Of what happened tonight?"

"No," she said. "I've got an interview to get ready for." She told him about the email from the *San Antonio Daily News*.

Lane blinked. "Oh, that's great. I'm right proud of you, sis. I hope you nail the interview. They'll be lucky to have you."

Evie's face warmed at the encouragement. "Thanks."

"Okay, I'll let you guys go," Lane said. "Thanks for everything, Carson, I mean it."

"No problem, man," Carson said.

Lane drove off, continuing toward Prosperity Ranch.

Evie's weight had been lightened once again by her brother's words. She wondered if she'd stayed in the small town and never left, if she would be as petty and small-minded as Jana and Deuce. She sure hoped not.

22

As CARSON PULLED INTO his parking space near his apartment building, he wondered if it was too late to text Evie. She'd gone completely silent since leaving Prosper. He'd texted her a couple of times, and she hadn't responded. He called her, too, but no answer. Carson had been tempted to reach out to her family, just to make sure they'd heard from her, and that she was okay. But he stopped himself every time he pulled up Holt's or Lane's number. And he wasn't about to get his grandad involved. No, Evie deserved her privacy.

Even if it was killing him. He'd felt the distance between them, growing and spreading, like a fissure in the earth widening with each passing hour.

He'd thought about going to her dorm building, knocking on her door, but now it was afterhours, anyway. She'd have to let him into the building, and why would she do that if she wasn't even texting him back? Climbing out of the truck, he gathered his things and walked up the stairs to his place. After going inside, he put away everything, then he switched off the lights and walked out onto the narrow balcony that overlooked a campus street.

His apartment had been a safe haven during his time

here, an escape from others with curious questions, a quiet place to study and to heal from losing his brother. But now, his apartment felt empty. And he felt alone.

Something that hadn't bothered him before meeting Evie.

He'd opened his heart to her the other night, and thankfully, she hadn't rejected him. She'd kissed him, and it was amazing, but then she'd left anyway. He got why she wanted to return early, to have some time to herself. Heck, he'd been relishing time to himself for two years. But now . . . the last thing he wanted to be was apart from her.

Carson pulled the phone from his pocket and texted her: *Hey. Back on campus. Pretty night.*

He waited a few minutes, but there was no reply. Okay, then. Maybe she was asleep, or in the shower, or . . . just not answering.

He sent another text: *If I don't see you before your interview, good luck. I'd love to hear about it.* SEND.

Nothing, again.

He strode back into his apartment, changed for bed, and spent the next two hours staring at the ceiling. Apart from the physical pull to be with Evie, to touch her, to smell her, to taste her, he racked his mind for how he could help her.

Carson wasn't even sure she understood the trauma she'd gone through from being bullied in school. She'd acknowledged it to him, but he sensed it was the first time she'd recognized it for what it was. And how did a person get over years of being made to feel less than?

If he hadn't had his brother and his granddad, Carson would have been a mess. His mom had never been in the picture, his dad left early on. Despite not having functioning or present parents, Carson had been blessed with love, acceptance, friends, and accolades.

What did Evie have? Love from her family, but had that been misguided as her brothers took on the protective role? Had they not seen what was happening to their own sister? Maybe that was why they were so protective about any guys who liked her. But they'd completely missed the ball on the popular girls group.

Even though Evie had opened up on some of the ways Jana treated her, Carson sensed there was probably more—a lot more. What was his role here? How could he help? Should he say something to her parents? Her brothers? What about her sister, Cara? Where did she fit into any of this? All Carson could tell was that Evie and Cara weren't close. As the only two sisters in the family, Carson was surprised, but what did he really know about functioning families?

Eventually, his tumultuous thoughts wore him down, and he slept a few hours.

Waking well before dawn, he decided to hit the campus gym. The team workout rooms would be open this time of the morning, and although they were relegated to the college athletes, they let Carson in. Nothing like lifting weights to get his mind off his spinning thoughts.

By the time he'd finished and completely worn his body out, he felt calmer. More focused. More . . . resilient, maybe? Whatever Evie decided about their relationship would be fine with him. Even if she wanted to end things just as they were getting started, he'd make it through fine. Maybe meeting her was the catalyst he'd needed to move forward with his life once again by opening himself up to new possibilities, new people, and new relationships.

Carson walked out of the gym into the rising dawn. The sun had yet to spill across the horizon, and no one was walking the campus yet. A few lights had flickered on in the buildings he'd passed. People were stirring, and soon, the day would be barreling forward. Carson had afternoon classes, so he'd spend the morning catching up on TA stuff for his professor.

He took the steps two at a time up to his apartment door, but stopped before reaching the landing.

Evie stood outside his door, wearing a sweatshirt and leggings. Her hair was in a snarled braid, and if he were to guess by the violet smudges beneath her eyes, she hadn't slept much last night.

Instantly, he wondered if she'd tried to text or call him, and he'd somehow missed it. But he knew he'd checked his phone as recently as ten minutes ago.

"Hey," he said in a soft voice, because her eyes were red-rimmed, and she looked like she was about to startle like a deer.

He ascended the final two steps until he was on the same level as she was. Evie still hadn't said anything, but her gaze was taking in the whole of him. He knew he was soaked in perspiration, and probably didn't smell too great, either.

"I didn't want to wake you," Evie said, her voice raw. "I didn't realize how early it was until I got here, and then I thought you were probably asleep, so I was trying to decide if I should knock."

Carson had no idea what had brought her here, or why she hadn't texted or called him back. But he didn't care. She was here now. "I'm not asleep," he said, moving closer. "In fact, I couldn't sleep, so I went to the gym."

"It's open this early?"

So, they were having a normal conversation before 6:00 in the morning?

"It is for athletes, and former athletes who have connections like me."

Her gaze again perused him, and he wondered what she was thinking. Why had she been crying?

"I messed up," she whispered.

Carson gazed at her, really looked. She was beautiful, even though she didn't wear a speck of makeup, and her eyes were red, and she was trembling. He hated that she was in pain, hurting, and he wanted to somehow fix it. *Tell me what to do,* he wished he could say.

"You didn't mess up," he said finally, wanting to pull her into his arms, but she'd ignored all of his communication for the past two days. So he was treading carefully here.

She sniffled and brushed at her eyes. "I did, and I'm sorry. Please don't hate me."

"Evie," he rasped. "I could never hate you." He wanted to reach out, to touch her, to somehow comfort her, but he didn't want to push her.

Her watery eyes met his. "Everything you did in Prosper was to help me. You confronted my brothers. You helped me realize the things that happened in school weren't right. You . . . believed in me."

Could a heart break while someone was still standing upright? "I still believe in you, sweetness."

"But I ghosted you, and you still texted me last night, and you're still . . . you." She motioned to his person. "You're the best guy I know other than my brothers—who could learn a lot from you. Even before you knew me, you actually cared, and you're . . . I don't know, maybe too good to be true."

The weight of her words was crushing his heart. How could she think so little of herself and so much of him?

"I thought that maybe I like you so much because you're my first kiss." Her cheeks flushed pink as she said this. "So I thought I'd come back to campus. Get some distance from my family, from Prosper, even from you. But it wouldn't go away."

When she didn't elaborate, Carson asked, "What wouldn't go away?"

"My feelings for you," she whispered, looking down as if she were embarrassed by her confession. "I thought it was a crush, but I've had a bunch of those, and you're way more than a crush."

Carson couldn't help smiling, even though he probably shouldn't. In fact, he wanted to laugh, then pull her into a tight hug. And when she was done crying, he'd kiss her senseless.

"That's the best thing I've heard in a long time, Evie—maybe ever," he said.

Her gaze snapped to his. "You don't hate me?"

"Why would I hate you?" he said, brushing her fingers with his.

"Because I'm a train wreck, and I'm painfully naïve, and I need someone to fight my battles for me."

He threaded their fingers together, and her hand tightened about his. "You're already fighting your own battles, Evie, I'm just carrying your sword when it gets a little too heavy to wield alone."

Her blue eyes filled with tears again, but this time, Carson didn't keep his distance. He leaned close and pressed a kiss on her forehead.

Evie's arms slipped around his waist, and she buried her face in his chest. She wasn't crying, but she was trembling. He drew her flush against him and rested his chin atop her head.

She clung to him for a long time, and Carson didn't mind in the least. He moved his hand along her back, stroking until her trembling stopped, and her breathing calmed.

"Want to come inside?" he asked after a long while.

No one had come up or down the stairs, but that could change soon.

"Okay," she murmured, then drew away.

She still looked like she'd been crying, but there was a softness about her expression now.

"And if you can wait a few minutes, I'll shower, and we can go get breakfast."

The smallest smile appeared. "You are kind of . . . fragrant."

Carson chuckled. "No doubt. Sorry about that."

She shook her head, her smile growing. "Don't apologize. You give the best hugs. Sweaty or not."

Carson would take her smile any day. He reached past her and unlocked his door, then pushed it open. He followed her inside, flipping on the lights. He didn't have a roommate; that had all changed when he transferred schools. He wasn't interested in keeping track of another person's social life or fighting for time to himself.

"Do you want water or anything?" he asked, moving to the fridge to pull out a couple of cold water bottles.

"Sure," she said as she paused in front of a collection of pictures he had on the end table in the living room. They were of him and Rhett.

Carson watched as she picked one up and examined it.

"You look a lot alike, but there are plenty of differences, too," she said in a soft voice.

"Yeah." Carson crossed to her, both water bottles in hand. He set the water on the end table, behind the photos. The photo in her hand was of his high school graduation. Carson was decked out in the graduation robe, and Rhett was in his classic cutoffs, a button-down shirt, and a tie for good measure. That was Rhett's way of dressing up.

The grin on Rhett's face made Carson want to both smile and cry at the same time. But here, standing with Evie and gazing at the photo together created a newer, different type of ache. His brother would never get to meet this woman—the one he was falling in love with, if she'd let him.

The fact that she was standing in his apartment was

definitely an improvement compared to the last couple of days.

Evie set down the graduation picture, then picked up the one of him and Rhett as younger kids. Both of them on horses. He remembered the day like it was last week, when his grandad had taken that photo. Right after, Rhett had dared Carson to a race. And they'd both urged their horses into a run, with Grandad hollering after them to slow down.

That was Rhett . . . always adding a challenge to everything.

"I can tell your brother loved you," Evie said, setting down the picture and turning to him. She slipped her hands to his waist. "And he was lucky to have such a great younger brother."

Carson gazed into the clear blue of Evie's eyes. "Thanks, sweetness."

She lifted a hand to his face, her fingertips soft against his skin. "I'm sorry I won't get to meet him."

Carson blinked against the burning in his eyes. "I'm sorry, too."

She raised up on her toes and pressed her mouth to his in a brief kiss. Before he could take it deeper, she drew away and patted his chest. "Yeah, go shower, handsome."

He smirked and grabbed one of the water bottles. "Make yourself at home," he said, then headed down the hall, his heart skipping about two paces ahead.

23

"YOUR RESUME IS IMPRESSIVE," Mr. Glen said, pushing up his glasses once again, then peering at her. "And you graduate in a couple of months?"

"Yes," Evie said, trying to tell herself to stop wringing her hands, or the director would notice.

Mr. Glen was the director of the graphics department for the *San Antonio Daily News*. It was early afternoon, and she'd spent the weekend working on some graphic mockups for the newspaper's website. She wasn't sure if she'd hand them over yet, but Mr. Glen had been a lot more responsive during her interview than she'd expected. Was this how he'd been with all the interviewees, though?

She knew that working for this company would be a dream come true, and her nerves were jumping all over the place because Mr. Glen seemed to genuinely be impressed.

Taking a deep breath, she reached for her computer bag and pulled out the portfolio she'd custom-made for the news-paper. Taking the design they already had on their website, which could frankly use an overhaul, she had upgraded and updated. Made it look more fresh and eye-catching. She'd printed out the new graphic designs, and now, she hoped she wasn't being too presumptuous.

But what better way to show her ideas than to use them on the existing newspaper?

"I brought some samples of my work," she said. "If you're interested, that is."

Mr. Glen's brows raised. "Let me see."

So she handed over the manila folder and watched as he lifted the cover.

He gazed at the first graphic.

Evie's heart thumped with nerves. She'd shown the graphics to Carson right before her interview, and he'd loved him. But he was her . . . boyfriend? She was pretty sure they were officially in that category now, and it made her heart sing. Although, she still didn't know how they'd make a long-distance relationship work. There was no way she'd let him turn down his grandad.

Mr. Glen turned the next page of her portfolio. "You've revamped our existing designs."

"Just as a demonstration," she said. "I wanted to give you specific examples for your newspaper."

Mr. Glen nodded and flipped through the rest of the graphics. Then he went through them again, more slowly this time. "Do you mind if I hang onto this, Ms. Prosper?" he asked. "We have a staff meeting this afternoon, and I'd like to present these."

Evie's mouth nearly dropped open. "You do? I mean, that's great. Sure, I have no problem with you showing them to the staff, if you think they might be interesting enough."

Mr. Glen closed the top cover of the folder. "They're excellent, and I must say, skipping any formalities, I'd like to offer you the position. Provided you can start as soon as possible after graduation. I'd love you to begin part-time as soon as you can, until you're able to go full-time."

Evie could only stare. He was offering her the job. Right now? "Oh, wow, thank you," she breathed. "What about the current person working in the position? Are they . . ."

"He's already on a leave of absence and won't be returning," Mr. Glen said. "I didn't post this in the job ad, but the opening is immediate. If you could check your schedule and get back to me by the end of the day and let me know what hours you can start working, that would be great. I can have you meet with HR tomorrow to get the paperwork started."

Evie nodded, as if she were following their conversation, although her mind was whirling. *She had the job.* The one that she'd only hoped for. "All right. I'll check my schedule, and, uh, call you? Or should I email?"

Mr. Glen shuffled around in one of his drawers, then handed over a business card. "This is my direct line. Leave a detailed message if I don't answer."

Evie's hands were shaking by the time she walked out of the director's office. She continued down the hallway, passing other offices, and her heart rate skipped with each footstep. She'd been offered the job. Her chest expanded, and she felt both elated and nervous.

Mr. Glen had seemed so impressed that maybe it was too good to be true. Maybe the other staff members wouldn't be as impressed. Still . . .

She pushed through the double doors of the building leading outside. Her pace only quickened when she saw Carson waiting for her by his truck, right where she'd left him. Although her car was now out of the shop, he'd offered to drive her, and she'd accepted.

No cowboy hat or boots today—he was back to looking like the typical college student. Well, there was nothing typical about Carson Hunt. He looked all hunky, with his broad shoulders and rolled-up sleeves exposing his sculpted forearms.

He was leaning against his truck, his eyes on his phone, but he looked up as she neared.

And she couldn't help but grin.

He pocketed his phone and straightened to his full height as he scanned her, his dark eyes on hers. His brows lifted, but before he could ask how her interview went, she threw her arms about his neck.

Carson chuckled and drew her close. "That good, huh?"

"They offered me the job on the spot," she breathed against his warm neck.

"Wow," he murmured. "But I'm not surprised, sweetness. Did you show them your sample designs?"

Evie drew away enough so that she was still in his arms, but she could see his smiling face. "I did. Mr. Glen said he was going to present them at the staff meeting this afternoon."

"That's amazing news. You're going to be a huge asset to them, you know."

Evie's stomach fluttered with nerves, and something else . . . something like guilt? Regret? She couldn't exactly identify it.

"Are you really so happy to get rid of me?" she said.

Carson slid his hand slowly across her back. "Are you trying to get rid of *me*?"

A smile tugged. "No . . ."

"Good," he said. "Because I'm not going anywhere." His mouth found hers, and the warmth of his kiss and the press of his body against hers made her head spin.

"Carson," she whispered against his mouth. "Wait."

He lifted his head.

"What do you mean you're not going anywhere?"

"I just got off the phone with my grandad," he said. "I officially turned down his offer. Maybe Prosper will work for us down the road, but right now, I'm here with you."

Evie drew in her breath. "You can't just . . ." But she could see in his eyes that he had.

"Evie, I'm in love with you," Carson said, his gaze boring into hers. "You're my number one, sweetness."

Tears burned in Evie's eyes. She wasn't sure why she was crying, because she felt insanely happy. "I don't know what to say," she said in a choked voice. "I can't believe you did that for me."

"Believe it," Carson said, his half-smile appearing. "I sent out a bunch of resumes early this morning, and I've already had two companies reply. So . . . it looks like we'll both be hanging out in San Antonio." He winked.

So she kissed him. They were in a public place, but Evie was good with that.

She'd never felt more secure, more at home, more comfortable and confident than she did when she was with Carson. She sighed as he drew back to gaze at her.

"Can you ditch a class and go celebrate?" he asked.

Evie gazed into the dark eyes of the man she was sure she'd fallen in love with. "What did you have in mind?"

"I kind of have a surprise."

Her brow wrinkled. "What have you been up to?"

"Come with me, and I'll show you."

She loved the way he was looking at her, the way his hands were resting on her hips, the way he was waiting for her approval. So she said, "Okay."

He opened the passenger door for her.

Once he climbed into his side, she reached for his hand, and he threaded their fingers together. Her heart was full, and her throat burned with emotion. Carson Hunt was planning on staying in San Antonio, and she could barely comprehend that. It was hard for her to argue with him, because she really wanted him with her. All the time.

When they reached a small Mexican restaurant, Evie said, "I've heard of this place, but haven't tried it yet."

"It's excellent," Carson said, flashing her a grin.

They walked hand in hand toward the restaurant, and Evie wondered why there weren't any other cars in the parking lot. "Does this place open late?"

"Not that I know of," Carson said, pulling open the front door for her.

She stepped inside to find a charming restaurant with bright colors and glittering lights overhead. There was a huge banner above the hostess stand that said *Congratulations.* Must be a party going on later? Before she could comment to Carson, a huge shout of "Surprise!" made her snap her head to the left.

People appeared above tables where they must have been crouching. Evie stared at her family members, her mom, dad, her brothers Lane and Holt. Macie and Ruby. And even Carson's grandad. Becca waved from her spot with a huge smile on her face.

"What are you all doing here?" Evie asked, and then two others stepped forward from the back of the group.

Her brother Knox, and her sister Cara.

"Oh my gosh!" Evie's eyes filled with tears. "What's going on?"

"We're celebrating your new job offer," her mom said in a wavering voice, coming forward to hug her.

Evie embraced her mom. "I don't understand, I just had my interview."

Her dad chuckled. "Seems that Carson thought you stood a good chance of getting the job."

Evie's mind was spinning in ten different directions. Cara moved toward her next. They hadn't talked much since Christmas, and their only communication had been on the family email or text strand. But Cara's smile was wide, and her dark blond hair in its signature knot. "Congrats, sis," Cara said before hugging Evie. "You're amazing."

Now, Evie couldn't swallow properly. She couldn't remember the last time her sister had given her a true compliment. There'd mostly been teasing.

"Hey, sis," Knox rumbled to her right.

And in an instant, she was hugging her brother, who'd only recently started interacting with family again. But somehow, he was here, for her. Even though Evie knew it had to be hard for him to see his ex-wife with Holt.

Knox's daughter was glued to his other side.

"My daddy came to see me," Ruby announced.

"He sure did," Evie said in a choked voice as she drew away from Knox and kissed the top of Ruby's head. She would never correct the little girl, because despite the limited time that Ruby saw her biological dad, she certainly idolized him.

"I can't believe you're all here," Evie must have said a dozen times as she hugged each person in turn. When she got to Becca, she said, "Were you in on this?"

She hadn't even seen Becca since coming back from spring break. Becca had said she'd be going straight to class when she got to campus that morning.

"I might have given Carson a few tips, but he did all the work."

Evie wiped at her cheeks, because it was impossible to hold back the tears. "How did you all get here so fast?"

"Speaking for myself, I flew in," Knox said, his tone amused.

Cara smiled. "Me, too."

Evie looked over at Carson, who was leaning against one of the tables, his arms folded. His knowing grin told her everything.

"We wanted you to know that we're so happy for your success," her mom said, "and that we're excited to hear all about your new career."

"Well . . ." Evie cleared her throat because emotion was starting to take over again. "They want me to start part-time as soon as I can, and full-time once I graduate."

"Good for you," Lane said, nodding. "I'm not surprised."

Macie stepped close and grasped her hand. "We're coming to visit you a lot," she said. "Ruby made me promise."

"I'd love that," Evie said, looking around at everyone. "And of course, I'll always be at Prosper for the holidays, or random weekends."

Her dad slung an arm about her shoulders and kissed the top of her head. "Whatever you decide, sweet pea."

"I thought *I* was your sweet pea," Ruby said in a clear voice.

Her dad chuckled. "You're both my sweet peas, how's that?"

"What about me?" Cara said with a laugh.

"Three sweet peas—anyone else interested?"

Becca raised a hand while grinning.

Everyone laughed, and Evie's gaze caught Carson's. He winked at her, and if the room wasn't filled with her family, she would have thrown herself into his arms. Instead, she mouthed, "Thank you."

He tipped an imaginary hat, one that she missed him wearing.

"Evie, darlin'." Holt set a hand on her shoulder. "I hope you know you can count on me for anything. And I'm sorry for any past hurts or misunderstandings."

"I know," Evie said in a quiet voice. "Thank you."

"Me, too," Cara said, joining them. "I haven't been the most supportive sister ever."

"You guys are going to make me cry some more."

Cara leaned in for another hug. "You got yourself a persistent man," she said with a smile. "He thinks you walk on water, and he would be right."

"Did he bribe you all or something?" Evie teased.

"No, but he's a straight shooter, in the best possible way," Cara said.

Her mom clapped her hands together from a few tables over. "All right, everyone, the buffet is just for us, and we have this place reserved for the next hour."

Evie stared at her mom, then swung her gaze to Carson.

He gave her a small satisfactory nod.

Evie crossed to him, no longer caring that every single member of her family was here. They wouldn't be in this room without Carson. She approached, and when she stopped in front of him, she placed her hands on each side of his face.

"How did you do all of this?" she asked, meeting that dark brown gaze of his.

"Lots of texting."

"I don't even know what to say, Carson," she said. "I can't even come up with the words to thank you."

Carson's gaze was steady on hers. "The expression on your face is my thanks, sweetness."

She kissed him then, lightly, but it sent her pulse zooming anyway. Slowly, she drew away from him, wondering how she got so lucky to meet Carson Hunt.

"I think someone wants to talk to you," he said.

Evie turned to see Mr. Hunt standing there, his cowboy hat in hand. "Congratulations, little lady," he said. "When Carson told me about your goal and how he felt about you, I couldn't push him out of Prosper fast enough."

Evie's face warmed. "Are you sure about this? I mean, Carson was looking forward to working with you—"

Mr. Hunt's rough hand rested on her arm. "Don't even go there, missy. You stole his heart, that's what. And a good woman is always the best part of any man's life. My happiness comes from seeing my only grandson happy, and I have you to thank for that."

Evie blinked back the tears in her eyes and stepped forward to hug his thin body. He patted her back, and it only made her smile.

When she drew away, she was pretty sure he had tears in his eyes as well.

"Let's eat," her dad announced, and they moved to the buffet on the other side of the restaurant.

Evie noticed employees at one end of the buffet, waiting to help if needed.

While everyone formed lines on both sides of the buffet, Evie was left alone with Carson for a few moments.

"I can't believe your grandad is being so great," she said.

"I told you he's a great guy," Carson said.

"So are you." Evie slid her hand into his, and they linked their fingers. Warmth zinged through her at the feel of his strong hand fitting with hers as if they were an unbreakable unit. With the rest of the family at the buffet, no one was paying them mind.

Carson's mouth lifted into a smile as his gaze soaked her in. "I like seeing you happy. And you deserve your family here to celebrate what you've accomplished."

"Are you trying to steal my heart, or something?"

Carson lifted his brows. "Is it working?"

She rested her free hand on his chest, right over his heart. "You stole it a while ago."

Carson leaned down until they were only a breath away from each other. "I like hearing that, sweetness." He kissed her gently, briefly, but with a thousand future promises.

Evie drew away with a sigh. She couldn't look away from his dark eyes, and she couldn't get enough of being around this man.

"I love you, Carson Hunt," she whispered.

His eyes widened, but then his smile only broadened. "I love you right back, Evie Prosper."

She was grinning, and her heart was soaring as Lane called out to them.

"Food's getting cold, you two," he said. "Better hurry before Knox and Holt finish off the entire buffet."

Her family members laughed, and Evie knew she was blushing by the time she turned to walk with Carson to the other side of the restaurant. Before meeting Carson, she'd been dead set against ever living in Prosper again, but now, she knew it might be a possibility. Someday.

With Carson at her side.

Heather B. Moore is a four-time *USA Today* bestselling author. She writes historical thrillers under the pen name H.B. Moore; her latest thrillers include *The Killing Curse* and *Breaking Jess*. Under the name Heather B. Moore, she writes romance and women's fiction. Her newest releases include the historical novels *The Paper Daughters of Chinatown* and *Deborah: Prophetess of God*. She's also one of the coauthors of the *USA Today* bestselling series: A Timeless Romance Anthology. Heather writes speculative fiction under the pen name Jane Redd; releases include the Solstice series and *Mistress Grim*. Heather is represented by Dystel, Goderich & Bourret.

For book updates, sign up for Heather's email list:
hbmoore.com/contact
Website: HBMoore.com
Facebook: Fans of H.B. Moore
Blog: MyWritersLair.blogspot.com
Instagram: @authorhbmoore
Pinterest: HeatherBMoore
Twitter: @HeatherBMoore

Made in the USA
Columbia, SC
03 September 2020

17728553R00120